EYE OF THE TIBER

Eye of the Tiger

EYE OF THE TIBER

S.C. Naoum

ENROUTE

En Route Books & Media
5705 Rhodes Avenue, St. Louis, MO 63109
Contact us at contactus@enroutebooksandmedia.com
Find En Route online at www.enroutebooksandmedia.com

LCCN: 2016960341

Cover design by TJ Burdick
Cover image credit: TJ Burdick and EOTT

Nihil Obstat:
You don't even know what this means,
so what do you care?

Hardback ISBN: 978-1-63337-146-0
Paperback ISBN: 978-1-950108-70-1
E-book ISBN: 978-1-63337-148-4

Printed in the United States of America

Contents

To my wife, Hilin, and my boy, Elijah, without whom this book would've still been completed

FOREWORD BY
MARK P. SHEA

"The opposite of 'funny' is not 'serious,'" said G.K. Chesterton. "The opposite of 'funny' is 'not funny.'"

Chesterton, one of the funniest, most serious, and profound thinkers who ever lived, then goes on to argue that, in fact, the power of humor relies completely on the seriousness of the subject. Ballistics, for instance, is just math and is not terribly funny by itself. Morality, on the other hand, is far more serious. And Chesterton makes their relationship to each other and to humor crystal clear when he remarks that, "We say of a man who can shoot his mother between the eyes at a hundred yards that he is a good shot, but not a good man."

Likewise, a joke about the pope wearing galoshes is funny precisely because the pope, not galoshes, is a serious subject. Take the pope out of the equation and galoshes are drained of all their

I

humor potential. Nobody ever walked through a Walmart giggling at a mere shelf full of galoshes. But ask, "How many skins of starving Asian laborers does it take to make a pair of Walmart galoshes?" (Answer: "Who cares? Check out these prices!") and such Swiftian humor again demonstrates that a joke—any joke at all—derives its power from deadly serious subjects, such as, for instance, a sin that cries out to heaven for vengeance—and the vengeance is often in the form of Swiftian humor.

The mention of sin brings us to something Americans have told each other for years: Never discuss politics, philosophy, money, or religion. And most especially, never joke about them. Fortunately, we do not obey such polite conversation killers for the very good reason that they are the four most interesting and serious issues in the world and grow in importance in that order.

Where would we be without political humor, or an American tradition of irreverence for our political class that has served beautifully in keeping in check our dangerous lust for secular messianism? It's hard to fall down in worship of Congresscritters when Mark Twain observes that politicians and diapers should be changed often—and for the same reason!

Likewise, philosophical discussions have been well-served by the constant remembrance brought to our minds by tenured clowns that "Ph.D" can often stand for "Piled higher and deeper." It was Cicero who said that there is no idea so absurd that some philosopher has not said it. And so Chesterton can crack us up in his hilariously funny little book, *St Thomas Aquinas: The Dumb Ox,* with this succinct analysis of the various schools of philosophy that have arisen in the modern era:

> Since the modern world began in the sixteenth cen-
> tury, nobody's system of philosophy has really cor-
> responded to everybody's sense of reality: to what,
> if left to themselves, common men would call com-
> mon sense. Each started with a paradox: a peculiar
> point of view demanding the sacrifice of what they
> would call a sane point of view. That is the one thing
> common to Hobbes and Hegel, to Kant and Bergson,
> to Berkeley and William James. A man had to be-
> lieve something that no normal man would believe,
> if it were suddenly propounded to his simplicity; as
> that law is above right, or right is outside reason,
> or things are only as we think them, or everything
> is relative to a reality that is not there. The modern
> philosopher claims, like a sort of confidence man,
> that if once we will grant him this, the rest will be
> easy; he will straighten out the world, if once he is
> allowed to give this one twist to the mind.

Chesterton's humor keeps a check on bad philosophy and
attests to the existence of Common Sense.

Likewise, where would we be without jokes about money—especially about money's abuse? From Scrooge McDuck's
swimming pool full of gold coins, to vaudeville hilarity as the
Marx Brothers make fun of dowager Margaret Dumont, to the
endless comedy of the Christian tradition dating right back to

the gag God pulls on the rich dude—(D'ja hear the one about the rich man who stored up treasure on earth? He died!)—we are chockablock with jokes and gags about money.

And this is supremely true in the world of religion. Many people are fearful of religious humor—and often rightly so. "Religious humor" that is blasphemous—whose object is the mockery of the All Good, All Beautiful, All Holy, All Righteous God—is evil. Period. Full stop. The name for it is Blasphemy. There is no excuse for it. God is not mocked. Because the purpose of humor is to see the incongruous and the disjointed, the broken and the false. It is not to mock what is good, or beautiful, or humble. A satire that targets the meek, the lowly, the wretched—that is to say, the crucified—is from hell.

But even blasphemy has a humorous irony that comes back to mock the blasphemer. It is this: blasphemy depends on the sacred, just as humor depends on the serious. "If you don't believe it," said Chesterton, "try blaspheming Thor."

Blasphemy is always directed at the God of Abraham, not Quetzalcoatl or Athena. Why? Because he's the real God and they do not exist. So a huge amount of such humor boils down to "God does not exist and I hate him!" The blasphemer complains that the Christian believes in magical thinking, and in the next breath complains that God doesn't magically eliminate war or famine.

But apart from blasphemy, there is plenty of religious humor that is totally legit. Even the Bible has some of it.

For instance, there is the hilarious burlesque of the tale of Jacob and his two wives, Leah and Rachel. One is used to reading Bible stories in a certain tone of voice, so that many Christians fulfill Voltaire's remark that God is a comedian playing to an audience afraid to laugh. But if you remove the yarn about Jacob and his wives from the atmosphere of stained glass and Gregorian chant in which it has been encased, this is the stuff of situation comedy and could easily be played for boffo laffs. The consummate liar who cheated his own brother out of his birthright gets diddled himself by his uncle Laban and, after working for seven years to get the girl, winds up instead with the man-hungry ugly sister in his bed the night after the wedding as Dad explains, "Oh! Did I forget to mention you have to marry Leah first? Silly me! So sorry! But you can have Rachel, no problem—after another seven years of labor."

Then there is the absurd competition between the sisters for position of Jacob's...generative faculties. Jacob, the alleged Master of the House, is dragged pillar to post by his demanding wives perpetually shouting, "It's my turn tonight!" One doesn't normally associate Scripture with a sort of French bedroom farce, but this tale definitely reads that way.

My favorite moment comes here:

> In the days of wheat harvest Reuben went and found
> mandrakes in the field, and brought them to his
> mother Leah. Then Rachel said to Leah, "Give me,
> I pray, some of your son's mandrakes." But she said
> to her, "Is it a small matter that you have taken away
> my husband? Would you take away my son's man-
> drakes also?" Rachel said, "Then he may lie with

you tonight for your son's mandrakes." When Jacob came from the field in the evening, Leah went out to meet him, and said, "You must come in to me; for I have hired you with my son's mandrakes." So he lay with her that night. (Ge 30:14–16)

Mandrakes were thought to be aphrodisiacs. That's why Rachel is so ticked and that's why Jacob, coming home from a long summer day of back-breaking work in the fields and looking forward to knocking back a few cold ones and watching some Monday night football before hitting the hay, is such a beleaguered doofus when he finds himself dragged off to the bedroom to, as the kids these days say, "put out" for Leah. You can practically picture The Man Who Would be Patriarch turning and giving a dead-eye stare into the camera like the principal at the end of *Ferris Bueller's Day Off*. Life just isn't 100% fun for him anymore. Thus do the whimsical ways of Providence result in judgments that are not stuck on to us externally by God, but are simply sin itself in fruition. Jacob's hilarious predicament is the result of Jacob's choice, and is, like everything else, for his good and ours. From this farce will come not just a sanctified-by-suffering Jacob, but the blessing that is the People of Israel.

And that's not the only moment of hilarity in Scripture. There's the yarn about Ehud, the left-handed Judge of Israel and the big fat tyrant Eglon. In a Marx Brothers movie, Eglon would be played by Sidney Greenstreet wearing spats and a top hat, and he'd be lighting his cigars with a hundred-dollar bill.

Ehud seeks a private meeting and shows himself unarmed by baring his left hip (the sword hip). In he goes and, when they are alone, he produces the sword concealed on his *right* hip and runs Eglon through so hard that the fat closes over the sword hilt. Then Ehud ducks out the window and runs off to rouse Israel to throw off their chains while the king's retainers stand around outside the royal chambers because they thought Eglon was sitting on the pot. By the time they figure out what's what, the revolt is in full swing and Israel is free. You can't tell me that story didn't crack everybody up when they told it around the campfire. ("How fat was Eglon? He was so fat that when he sat around the palace he sat *around* the palace!")

The Jewish and Catholic traditions have likewise been a bottomless source of humor. The Jewish tradition of self-criticism that goes all the way back to the prophets has spawned an entire genre of self-deprecating humor ("How many Jewish mothers does it take to change a lightbulb?" Answer: "That's alright. I'll just sit here in the dark. Don't mind me.") And the Jewish history of persecution has likewise spawned an entire tradition of defense against oppressors through satire: ("Rabbi, what's a good prayer for the Tsar?" "May God bless and keep the Tsar—far away from us.")

Catholics follow in that tradition with a gigantic cataract of jokes and gibes, vast numbers of which are directed at themselves and their foibles, and an equal number directed at the crazy world in which they live. Tertullian got boffo laffs when he described the heretic Marcion as having, "a pumpkin, instead of a brain." Augustine's ruthless assessments of his own sins included the insightful witticism that his prayer, for years, was, "O Lord, make me chaste. But not yet." St. Teresa of Avila could even, with piety and the frankness of a saint, make funny replies to God in her prayers, as when God told her, "This is how I treat all my friends" after she was unceremoniously dragged through a muddy river and deposited on the bank when her saddle strap gave way. Her tart reply: "Then, Lord, it is no wonder you have so few." Sts. Thomas More and Philip Neri could be pretty funny too. (More, at the bottom of the scaffold whose summit feature the block on which he would lose his head, said, "See me safely to the top and I will shift for myself coming down.")

And we can't forget St. Lawrence, who, confronted with a pagan bigwig looking for the Secret Treasures of the Roman Church, said, "Coming right up!" and presented him with a motley crew of beggars, blind men, widows, children, and other Undesirables and said, "What else can I do for you?" Then, as he was being roasted alive by his Roman torturers for this joke, Lawrence reportedly remarked, "You can turn me over. I'm done on this side now." That is what you call "chutzpah." Fittingly, the folk piety of the Catholic communion has preserved his sassy, finger-in-the-eye cockiness toward persecutors and death by making him the patron saint of cooks, tanners—and comedians. I don't care who you are, that's funny.

Not just saints and theologians have been funny (and, by the way, I am morally certain nobody has ever written those words in that order before). Shakespeare, Chaucer, and Bocaccio were all Catholic funny guys. There were whole subcultures

VIII

of Irish, Italian, and German immigrants who brought their Catholic humor to America and filled vaudeville, radio, and television with it. These days, Bob Newhart and Jim Gaffigan are Catholic comedians, along with a host of others who were raised Catholic (Jimmy Fallon, Bill Murray, Stephen Colbert, Conan O'Brien, Brian Regan, etc.), and the movies are full of lines written by brilliantly funny people whose Catholic faith is grist and inspiration.

Samer (S.C.) Naoum stands in that tradition too. He has a keen sense of our foibles as human beings. And he has had a jolly time lampooning, not Holy Church and not God, but we extremely fallible members of that Church who are the very breakable jars of clay in which God has chosen to place his treasure. This includes every member of the Church from the pope to the dog catcher. I can't tell you how many times I have burst out laughing at the latest edition of *Eye of the Tiber* when it pops up in my feed. Treasured moments have included the announcement—following a big slide show projected on the face of St. Peter's Basilica in celebration of Earth Day and the encyclical *Laudato Si*—that the Vatican will have a permanent display of Microsoft screensaver bubbles projected on St. Peter's. I also loved "Priest Magician Performs Folk Mass Illusion: Makes Parishioners Disappear" and "New DC Comics 'Benedict v. Francis: Dawn of Mercy' Getting Terrible Reviews."

In the pages of this book you will meet the manufacturers of Catholic Happy Talk who want to change Holy Days of Obligation to Holy Days of Opportunity, the baffled parishioner not sure of whether to mourn or rejoice at the sight of a

Resurrexifix, the 17-year-old homeschooled boy who figured out the Trinity while his mom combed his hair, and the OCD parishioner who makes sure all the missals are upright in the pews. These people are familiar to us. Many of them *are* us, including a writer I know with a rare species of bird nesting in his beard. Our laughter is not one of scorn but of a sort of rueful familiarity. Samer Naoum makes you laugh and say "Ouch" at the same time.

Then again, he just comes up with stuff that's daffy just for the fun of it: "Statue in Cathedral of Our Lady of the Angels Wondering Why Everyone Keeps Laughing at It" is a bit off the wall. And one of my personal favorites is "Clown at Circus Mass Reprimanded for Honking Sanctus Horn at Wrong Part of Consecration."

I could go on and on, but you get the idea. *Eye of the Tiber* has that odd Monty Python quality of coming up with jokes you like repeating even after everybody knows them. And the best part is, this material is new and it's just scratching the surface. There's plenty more where this came from. Giggle away, share it with a friend, become a fan, and when you are done, demand some more—or should I say, Samer.

No. I'm not sorry I did that.

"And I will make them eat the flesh of their sons and their daughters, and every one shall eat the flesh of his neighbor in the siege and in the distress, with which their enemies and those who seek their life afflict them."

—Jeremiah 19:9

Mass

Local pastor Fr. Ned Sterling has stopped and restarted Mass fifteen times in the past three minutes, witnesses at St. Gemma Galgani Catholic Church are reporting. Thomas told EOTT, "I always get in to church about five minutes into the homily, which happened today, but then, once Father Sterling saw me walk in, he stopped talking, walked to the back of the church and processed in again."

Quick-Thinking Parishioners Rush Altar
to Assist Lone Priest

Parishioners of St. Raymond Catholic Church in Culver City, California were forced to jump into action during Mass early Monday morning when it appeared that only one priest would be available for the consecration.

According to sources at the scene, parishioners went into a frenzy when it appeared that visiting priest Fr. Bryce Carbone was close to saying the words of consecration all by himself.

"Our regular pastor, Fr. Ed, usually invites us all to gather and encircle the Lord's table during consecration," said longtime parishioner Donna Fullwood, before reassuring reporters that Carbone was doing well despite his brush with Mass without liturgical participation. "All I can say is it was a close call. I know a few parishioners are a little shaken up thinking of what could've happened if they hadn't been able to participate. All's well that ends well, though."

56-year-old Fullwood went on to recount the story of how twenty or so quick-thinking parishioners rushed into action as Carbone prepared to consecrate the bread and wine without a single layman there to assist him. "We all looked at each other like 'Oh no,' then rushed to the altar as quick as we could and surrounded it. Then we all lifted one hand each in the concelabratory way. It was amazing how fast everyone moved to assist Fr. Bryce. I'm sure he's really thankful. Maybe they'll make a movie about it one day, like *Zero Dark Thirty* or something."

Report: Some 2nd Century Roman Christians Hated Latin Mass Because It Was Said in the Vernacular

A letter written by an anonymous early Roman Christian was unearthed at the base of the Palatine Hills earlier this week, revealing that many Christians living in Rome at the time hated the Latin Mass because it was being said in the vernacular.

The letter, which scientists are dating back to the early 2nd century, reveals much angst and division in the early Church between those who believed it was acceptable to use the vernacular during Mass, and those who believed that Aramaic ought to have been the only acceptable language, as the use of it reportedly dates back to the first Mass said by Jesus Christ.

"The letter is absolutely remarkable," said Eugene Cardoza, who headed the team that unearthed the letter. "It was written by a frustrated Christian to a friend, in response to an angry letter about the expanding use of the vernacular during Masses in Rome. I think the most fascinating thing to learn was that while Christians were being persecuted by the government, they decided to squabble over language instead of coming together to fight for their right to religious freedom."

Although only a portion of the letter has been found, what remains sheds much light on issues that faced more traditional circles of Christians in Rome. An excerpt of the letter found has been graciously translated by the Church's *Office of Linguistic Studies* and has been transcribed below.

Dearest Brother,

Greetings be upon you, and upon you be greetings. May the peace and grace of our Lord Jesus Christ, from whom all good things come, bless you and your home. From your dispatch, I have learned the unsettling news that many of our brethren in Rome are irritated that some are beginning to use vernacular during the Lord's Supper. I myself, in common with many others, was full of sorrow when your dispatch arrived with the unsettling news that the holiness and beauty of Aramaic has been usurped by Latin; for you have given me sad news that this new vernacular Mass is doing much dishonor to the traditions that have been passed down to us by the Lord and the apostles themselves. I, therefore, must admonish you to stay clear from those who uphold such scandal to the Supper of the Lord, and in all due diligence must inform you that this new order of the Lord's Supper is an abomination at best. Though your private letter to me contained a somewhat slight expression of your angst, I can assure you that it gave me pleasure that you were grieved, for, by grievance you have proven yourself to the Lord. More importantly, you have proven yourself a true Christian, more Christian than Sixtus, for there is nothing in which I habitually find greater satisfaction and true holiness than in bitterness and hostility. I am overjoyed that you propose to write a letter to Sixtus in all capital letters and with an abundance of exclamation marks. I also write to inform you that in response to this news, I propose now to make bishop of you, as well as Alexander, Aurelius, and our beloved Lucias, whose minds I trust are in accord with our own. This, I shall do without the permission of Sixtus. For he, it seems, has fallen in to grave sin when he gave ear to a number of Jews to assist in reforming the Lord's Supper during his meeting last month with fellow bishops in his territory. I shall end this letter by telling you that our new "society" shall ever and always pretentiously look down upon those that..."

New Study Shows 99% More Catholics Attend Holy Day of Obligation When Called Holy Day of Opportunity

A new study out today by the *National Catholic Research Company* (NCRC) says that 99% of Catholics are more likely to attend Mass on a Holy Day of Obligation if it's called a "Holy Day of Opportunity."

President of the NCRC, Robert Donavan, told EOTT that while it's the same Mass and obligation, most people did not like being told what to do.

"The fact is that if people believe that they're being invited to, as opposed to forced to, come to Mass, almost every Catholic will in fact find the time."

The study also revealed that 100% of fallen away Catholics and nominal Catholics were likely to make it to Mass on a Holy Day of Obligation if told not to attend by the pastor.

Monday Morning Priest Would've Said
Mass Completely Different

After having attended Mass yesterday evening, Denver native and layman Jeffrey Baines went on his public access television show *Clerical Primetime* this morning to criticize his parish pastor, Father Roger Manning, for quitting midway through Mass.

Manning had nearly a quarter of his usual attendance at his Sunday evening Mass. "It was a really empty Mass," a worked up Baines screamed at the camera after attending what he called the most "embarrassing" showing at a Mass he had ever seen. "That not a lot of people showed up was one thing. That was to be expected. But to throw in the towel during that disastrous homily...that's another thing."

In an interview with EOTT this morning, Manning defended himself saying that the Mass was "not embarrassing at all." "I would never use that word. The word 'embarrassing' is an insulting word, to tell you the truth."

But many people who attended the Mass said that sometime midway through the homily, Manning had seemingly "thrown in the chasuble."

"It wasn't just Manning," one parishioner said when interviewed on *Clerical Primetime*. "The Mass is a team effort. The priest runs the show, but everyone from the deacon, who only high-fived six people during the sign of peace, to the eucharistic ministers, who were slow and lazy in distributing communion, were to blame. There's always next Mass, and Father

Manning is such a great priest...but at this point we really need to start considering Manning's legacy as a priest."

New Eco-Friendly Church Using Biodegradable Chalice

Speaking to an assembly of Catholic priests in London yesterday, Pastor of St. Philip Neri Catholic Church in nearby Chigwell, England, Fr. Timothy Rooney, announced yesterday that he would be transforming his church into a more eco-friendly environment, and encouraged those gathered to follow his lead.

"Parishioners considering our churches as a place to pray will ask about our green initiatives. It is important for us to reassure them that we are pursuing practices for a greener environment," Rooney said, as he pulled out the new biodegradable chalice he would be using for Mass. "Gone are the days when we used precious metals for chalices. Just imagine how many wasted, jeweled chalices litter and pollute the earth ever since we switched to glass chalices. It's sickening. We are essentially sending a mixed signal every time we say Mass using a precious metal. We're saying, 'Welcome and thank you for coming, Jesus...and now behold as we destroy your earth.'"

But biodegradable chalices aren't the only "green" religious supplies being used at St. Phillip Neri Catholic Church. Rooney went on to explain that he would be replacing all religious images with the recycling symbol, or an image of the earth with the word *Environment* written beneath it.

"The fact is, everyone gets the point that Jesus died for us. But people obviously aren't getting the point that this earth is dying for us as well. Must everyone or everything die to prove their love for us?"

Unimaginative Priest Celebrates Themeless Mass

Citing a lack of time and energy, as well as feeling the "total absence of the liturgical muse," local pastor Fr. Mike Conway spent close to no time at all this week considering a theme for this Sunday's Mass.

"I remember just ten years ago when I could come up here with my jeans and piece of straw in my mouth for a Hillbilly Mass, before changing into a Barney costume for my Children's Mass," Conway said, fondly describing a time when the uncharted landscape of Mass themes seemed as boundless as the sea. "Ah, yes...those were days of adventure; days when a priest could become a sort of clerical Columbus, voyaging his own imagination for the most absurd and inventive themes to keep the Mass from getting stale. Indeed, those were the days. But alas, after so many Clown Masses, Superhero Masses, Meme Masses, Luau Masses, World Cup Masses, and Atheist Masses, it seems as though the liturgical muse has hidden himself from mine eyes."

Conway went on to say that he was not the only priest having trouble coming up with new themes, and that many had been dipping into old "routines" for years now. "So this week, unfortunately, my flock is going to just have to sit and put up with me wearing vestments and reading from the Missal. Ohh...you know what? Maybe I can have a reverent theme. That might be funny."

At press time, Conway was preparing a Latin themed Mass, in

which everything would be said in Latin, and everyone would be dressed as centurions.

Dumbstruck Congregation Listens in Awe As "Judgmental" Pastor Delivers Sound Homily

Listening in shock and horror as a visiting priest delivered what many believed to be a judgmental homily earlier this morning, many parishioners at Sacred Heart Catholic Church were traumatized after listening to what some called "the most sound homily they had ever heard."

"It was disgusting," one parishioner, Debbie Locke, told EOTT. "This is a church for goodness sakes." Others also voiced their concerns saying that such filth should never be spoken anywhere, let alone in a church. "This is the house of God!" parishioner Bob Woodward said. "Is there no place left in the world where we can avoid hatred, injustice, judgment, and sound Catholic doctrine?!"

According to Woodward, a world that "did not allow for a woman's right to choose, or for two men to love one another" was not a world deserving of the King of Kings. The baffled and furious parishioner went on to explain how he was forced to flee Denver years ago after noticing a more prevalent and uncomfortable trend of sound homilies coming from several pulpits around the diocese. "The Bishop was doing nothing about it, so I fled with my family from Denver so that we could get away from that kind of critical and unwelcoming attitude. I chose to flee so that my Catholic children could grow up in a world that is accepting of all things...even if they're not even remotely close to being in the same vicinity of being in line with Catholic teaching."

Priest Who Struck Breast during Sanctus Was Having Heart Attack Unbeknownst to Parishioners

Sources from St. Gregory Catholic Church are now confirming that, although their pastor was having a heart attack right in front of their eyes during last weekend's vigil Mass, no one had a clue because it "looked like he was beating his chest because of the Sanctus."

"We had no clue," parishioner Tim Gerard told EOTT. "We just thought he was getting more into the Mass this week than usual."

Another parishioner explained to EOTT about how vigorously Fr. Donny O'Brian was beating his chest during the Sanctus.

"I couldn't believe how into the Mass someone could get. He was beating and sweating and he had gotten all pale. I suppose I should've known something was wrong when he started chewing Advil and asking for someone to call 9-1-1. I just thought that was another new change in the Mass or something. Like Jesus and the angels are 9-1-1 and he was asking us to call upon some sort of spiritual ambulance to help save our ailing souls. I guess I screwed up there."

Woman Criticizes Jesus for Giving Apostles Communion in the Hand

Lorenza Matthews expressed disappointment last week when she noticed that, according to the Gospel accounts of the Last Supper, Jesus "gave" the Apostles his Sacred Body and told them to "take" it.

"I'm a bit scandalized that our Lord would brush aside the traditional practice of Communion on the tongue while kneeling." When asked about her frustration, Matthews added, "We use our hands to commit all kinds of sins, and it's just so disrespectful to just stand there with our hands out, as if we're beggars asking for charity from God or something." She continued, "But what sins could we ever commit with our tongues? And what gesture could be more respectful than sticking them out to welcome our Eucharistic Lord into our hearts?"

Friends and fellow parishioners noted that this stance is a consistent one with Lorenza, equal or greater in importance than any other in her life. "Communion in the hand is not the way I grew up, and it's just not respectful. Jesus needs to realize that." She concluded, "We can't go around making our personal preferences equal to God's holy law."

Seating for Mass Turns Chaotic after
Ushers Call in Sick

Mass at St. Alphonsus Parish in Bowie, Maryland quickly turned chaotic earlier this morning after all eight ushers called in sick with the flu.

66-year-old Herman Wible, who was one of the first to arrive for the early-morning liturgy, said, "At first I thought that the ushers would soon arrive, so I just waited outside. But by 6:55, as more people came, it became clear that no ushers were showing up. We didn't know what to do. No one knew which door to go through, much less which pew to sit in." Another parishioner, Katherine Warfield, told EOTT that she had never witnessed such a scene in "all her years." "People were sitting on top of each other...others were sitting on their heads, and one guy was sitting backwards. I even saw one poor woman screaming because six other people were sitting on top of her. I wanted to tell them that the rest of the pew was empty but, without an usher there to confirm that the seats weren't being held for some group, I said nothing and just prayed for her."

No Laity Found to Bring up Gifts to Altar; Consecration Delayed Two Hours

Pastor of St. Dwenden Catholic Church in Toronto, Canada, Ben Gregory, was forced to postpone the consecration for nearly two hours early Sunday morning after lead usher, Kevin Sarkosy, was unsuccessful in locating anyone willing to bring up the bread and wine for the presentation of the gifts at Mass.

"Obviously the presentation is as important to the Mass as the consecration is...everyone knows that," Sarkosy told EOTT as he and three others searched, frantically, for a willing family to present the gifts. "In fact, I go as far as to say that the laity's role in presenting the gifts is as important as Father Gregory's is in consecrating it. Without Mary's *Fiat*, after all, there is no Jesus to be born; and without the laity's *Fiat* in presenting, there is no bread to become Jesus...if you think about it like that."

Sarkosy went on to report that everyone was acting very peculiar as he approached them to ask whether they would be interested in participating. "They all had their heads down...like they were praying or something," Sarkosy chuckled. "I mean, my wife and I would've done it, of course, except that we had the money baskets to carry."

Scientists Test Effects of Novus Ordo on Longtime Sedevacantist

Attempting to explain the physical and emotional toll that an average Sedevacantist would endure during a Novus Ordo, students at UCLA have recently begun tests on 54-year-old Sedevacantist John Weiss of Glendale, California.

"Thus far the results have been quite fascinating," Head of the Department of Sciences at UCLA Dr. William Manders told EOTT. "We began by strapping Mr. Weiss in a pew beside a man wearing shorts. After placing eye clips over his eyes to keep his lids from shutting, we had a woman wearing a tank top sit directly in front of him. You could immediately see that Mr. Weiss was beginning to sweat and was becoming extremely anxious...almost agitated."

With the help of the UCLA Theatre Department, Manders began a battery of tests on Weiss, which included a staged Novus Ordo.

"It appears as though the moment Mr. Weiss runs across anything remotely sentimental during the Mass, such as a smile on the priest's face, his heart rate begins to rise and he begins to mutter what seem to be bitter remarks. At one point Mr. Weiss became quite physical when one of our mock parishioners went to hold his hand during the Our Father. Luckily, we already had placed a taser collar on him, which we were quick to use."

One department faculty member said she became worried for the "poor soul" when the mock congregation, led by a bearded, ponytailed guitarist, began to sing "One Bread, One Body."

"He was beginning to twitch for goodness sakes, and I knew then that that was about as much as I could endure. By the time I left he was foaming at the mouth. Don't they have Sedevacantist mice they could test on?"

Area Baptist Church Runs out of
Welch's 100% Grape Juice for Communion

Pastor Kyle Sandera of Newlife Baptist Church in San Diego, California says that an unanticipated large crowd at Sunday service this past weekend depleted their Welch's 100% Grape Juice reserve before everyone was able to partake in the breaking of bread.

"We honestly just didn't expect that that many people would show," Sandera told EOTT. "Thirty people! It's our first year as a church, so I guess we're still learning."

One Newlife member, who asked to remain anonymous, claims that the 24-ounce bottle of Welch's 100% Grape Juice used for communion was half empty before the service had even begun.

"One of Pastor Kyle's kids got his hands on the bottle and was suckin' that thing down like he'd never tasted a symbolic representation of Christ's blood before. It's alright though," he continued, "it doesn't say anywhere in scripture that the symbol of our Lord's blood has to be Welch's... That would be ridiculous."

The man went on to tell EOTT that he was actually glad to see the grape juice finish before it got to him, and that he liked the replacement juice he received, jokingly calling it the "Capri Sun Sacrament." "You know...nothing like sitting there in our church in the air-conditioned boardroom at the Bay Front Motel 6 drinking a Capri Sun to help recall the Last Supper."

XXX

Purr-Iest Says Meow Culpa at Wrong Part of Cat Mass

Speaking to his congregation after the 9:00 a.m. Cat Mass yesterday, pastor of St. Francis of Assisi Catholic Church in Cat-alina Island, Fr. Bojangles, apologized for having said the Meow Culpa at the wrong part of Mass.

"I've never done that before," a baffled Bojangles told those gathered as he licked his paw over and over again before wiping his face clean. "I'm taking this kinda hard right now be-claws I'm a purr-fectionist."

While many cats in attendance called the mistake "claw-ful," others said that he was fur-tunate to not have made the mistake during the consecration.

"I personally thought it was hiss-terical," said long time parishioner of St. Francis Catholic Church, Caterina Ivanovna, as she raised her butt in the air to stretch. "We need to give Fr. Bojangles some paw-sitive reinforcement right now. I know he's beating himself over this one."

Man Dressed as Tabernacle at Halloween Party Ignored; Is Moved to Corner of Room

According to reports from several eyewitnesses moments ago, 27-year-old Austin man Emmanuel Dickens, who showed up to a Halloween party dressed as his favorite tabernacle, was promptly ignored and escorted to the corner of the room.

The party's host, Thomas Martin, told EOTT that having the man there was "for some reason just kinda putting a damper on the fellowship thing" he was going for.

"It's not necessarily that he's not wanted at the party," Martin said. "It's just that it's a bit awkward when everyone's trying to catch up and chit-chat, and he's just standing there not saying anything." Kimberley Wilson, who also attended the party, reported that she had a pleasant, though brief, conversation with Dickens, but that it was difficult to focus on what he was trying say.

"Well, no one else was talking to him, and he was relegated to the corner like he had some kinda disease. I thought I'd say hello, but it's kinda hard when everyone's talking so loud. Not to mention the David Haas Pandora station blaring in the background. I couldn't understand anything he was trying to say."

At press time, Martin was considering moving Dickens to another room altogether.

Lazy Man Not Helping to Put up Kneeler

A source out of St. Ulric Catholic Church in West Bloomfield, Michigan confirmed Sunday that parishioner Alexander Ramsey had not lifted a finger to assist in putting up or down the kneeler for the consecration.

"I can see he's a really big guy, but come on... I know he can reach down a foot," the source told EOTT. "Or just *use* your foot, for goodness sakes. It's not difficult...look," he said, going on to show how it was done, putting it up then down, then up again and down again. "Oh, how hard and straining that was," he said, mockingly, as he wiped invisible sweat from his forehead.

"Look, I'm not an idiot," the source later confirmed. "I know exactly what's going on here. Every time I reach down for the kneeler he moves his hand toward the kneeler as if he was just about to do it. It's fine. He may think he can pull one over on me, but he can't pull one over on God."

Elderly Woman Mumbling Words of Consecration from Pew

Parishioners at the Catholic parish of St. Adelaide let out a sigh of relief during Mass this morning after parishioner Veronica Hough validated the consecration by mumbling the words of institution along with the priest.

Many parishioners reported to EOTT after the Mass that they were afraid 74-year-old Hough had forgotten her duty as co-consecrator after parish priest Fr. Ronald Sterling began the consecration without her.

"There were a couple seconds there where Fr. Ronald was up at the altar saying the words of consecration all by himself. I remember looking over to my wife and my wife looking at me wondering why the heck Veronica wasn't co-consecrating like she always does. But then she started and you could see everyone in the church let out this collective sigh. My wife reminded me after the Mass how close we had come to receiving only half-consecrated Eucharist. Scary."

Groundbreaking New Drug Helps Parishioners Cope with Devastating Sound of Church Band Playing during Mass

A new anti-anxiety drug called Xanoft is now being offered to parishioners as young as five years old to help curb the devastating effects of the sound of bad church music, scientists are reporting.

The drug, which many parishioners are calling a "miracle," is said to be able to "soften" the senses to the sounds of guitar, tambourine, and other instruments when played inside of a church.

"It's the most amazing drug on the market," said local Catholic Debbie Kang, who has been using a trial version of the drug for a month. "I used to seizure every time the church band started playing. But now I'm able to stay conscious so I can curse the members of the band under my breath."

Another Xanoft user, Logan Thomas, told EOTT that he was on the verge of leaving the Church for SSPX before learning about Xanoft. "I just couldn't take it anymore. But now with Xanoft I'm able to sit through an hour of the most ungodly music during Mass without having to go to confession right after."

Local Parish Abandons Mass So as Not to Distract from Parishioners' Conversations

Local pastor Fr. Robert Dunn reported to his congregation in the parish newsletter this morning that beginning the week after Easter, all Masses were to be replaced by an hour of straight-up fellowship.

This news came as no shock to many of the parishioners who said that the Mass had been disintegrating for some time before the announcement was made official.

"Oh yeah, we saw this coming a mile away," said 43-year-old parishioner Jacob Bryant. "I mean, about forty to fifty minutes of the Mass is solely dedicated to the sign of peace anyway, so when I read about the no Mass thing, it was basically him telling us that he was simply doing away with ten to twenty minutes of Mass time."

In the newsletter, Dunn said that he had come to the decision after witnessing "the damage praying was doing to good quality fellowship time."

"I really shouldn't even say that praying was doing damage to fellowship time, because in all reality, fellowship is the highest form of praying, if you know what I'm saying."

At press time, we still don't know what he's "saying."

"Extraordinary Mass Should Not Be the Norm," Extraordinary Minister of Holy Communion Reporting

Extraordinary Minister of Holy Communion Ernest Robbins is reporting to friends and family that the Extraordinary Form of the Liturgy "should never become the norm," but that it should "remain true to its name...extraordinary."

"I don't know...I just feel that Vatican II helped us move into a new era in the Church, and I guess I just don't wanna see us move backwards," Robbins declared to anyone and everyone listening, going on to explain how the Spirit of Vatican II has helped to reshape the proper form of the Mass. "Where just a few decades ago I had to passively receive Jesus, I can now boldly *give* Jesus, just as He so boldly gave Himself to us. The Extraordinary Mass is a roadblock to my participation in the giving action of the Lord. And I mean, isn't it just common sense that the Extraordinary form should remain extraordinary?" Robbins laughed. "Say it with me...'extra...ordinary.'"

At press time, Robbins was drafting an email to Steve Greydanus of *Decent Films,* asking him to begin a petition to HBO to have them stop airing *The League of Extraordinary Gentlemen.*

Priest Has next Sunday's Crappy Homily All Sketched Out

According to sources close to local priest Fr. Donny Irving, the longtime pastor of St. Genevieve Catholic Church told parishioners that he had completed sketching out next week's crappy homily.

58-year-old Irving told many of his parishioners via email that his homily about the feeding of the multitude was all sketched out and that he was planning to begin writing it within the next hour or so, so that he could finish it a few minutes later.

"Oh this one's a good piece of unintelligent fluff," he told his parishioners as he longingly gazed at his hastily written sketch on a napkin he used at the local coffee shop to sketch the homily. "I simply cannot wait for Sunday when I can preach this utter and complete pile of bullshit."

Irving went on to say that many of his fellow priests would be so envious, seeing as how he at least spent *some* time on his homily, as opposed to simply regurgitating outdated, unoriginal hippie crap he learned in the seminary.

At press time, Irving was in the process of sketching out what will eventually be a painting of Jesus feeding the multitude called, "Sharing is Caring."

"**O**h this one's a good piece of unintelligent fluff," he told his parishioners as he longingly gazed at his hastily written sketch on a napkin he used at the local coffee shop to sketch the homily. "I simply cannot wait for Sunday when I can preach this utter and complete pile of bullshit."

New Report Shows That Homilies Were Never Meant to Be That Good Anyway

A new report out today claims that homilies were not ever really meant to be that good in the first place.

The report put out by the Vatican says that, although a number of homilies in the past may show what some believe to be clear evidence of being well thought out and written sermons, those homilies were, in fact, unintentional.

"What we found is that, while some ancient homilies we studied were well written, that almost all of them were written by men who obviously meant for them to be used as a means to purge temporal sins," said Chief Homily Expert Ronaldo Di Stefano. "Some of the priests were trying to use elevated, deep, and truly insightful language to make their parishioners suffer so as to purge sins. The problem, we know now, is that Catholics then were a little more educated and spiritual than they are now. They were actually leaning about their faith and loving it."

Di Stefano went on to say that while priests long ago attempted to make their parishioners suffer through their homilies by means of insightful language, they were going on about it in the wrong way.

"The fact is that, while their hearts were in the right place, the means by which they attempted to make crap out of a perfectly good gospel was off. It was only in the 1960s that priests first truly started to learn about the art of shitty, fluffy homilies."

Priest Restarts Mass Every Time
Late Parishioner Arrives

Local pastor Fr. Ned Sterling has stopped and restarted Mass fifteen times in the past three minutes, witnesses at St. Gemma Galgani Catholic Church are reporting.

The news comes just minutes after late-comer Jonathan Thomas arrived to Mass, prompting Sterling's fifteenth Mass stoppage.

"I was kinda annoyed, actually," Thomas told EOTT. "I always get in to church about five minutes into the homily, which happened today, but then, once Father Sterling saw me walk in, he stopped talking, walked to the back of the church and processed in again."

Another parishioner, Joy Belmonte, who witnessed the incidents, reported that the most painful part of the experience was not having to sit in church for three hours, but was in fact having to hear the entrance hymn fifteen times.

"Come *on*," Belmonte said. "I know the Church is against suicide, but how many times can someone listen to "Sing a New Song" without contemplating ending one's own life?"

Innovative Priest Attempts to Institute
Communion under Three Species

Just hours after Mass Sunday morning, local pastor Fr. Jerome Dickenson reported that he believed his attempt to transubstantiate a third species during the Mass had completely failed.

"I just thought it'd be cool to have another substance to throw in there. Really hope God didn't notice," Dickenson reported. "Listen…so many cool things are happening with the Church, I just thought this too might fall through the cracks and be allowed."

Dickenson later admitted that he should've known it wouldn't have worked when the true Body, Blood, Soul, and Divinity of Christ alone was more often than not enough to bring Catholics to Mass.

Area Parishioner Reporting He's Not Gay; "Ain't Gonna Hold Another Man's Hand during the Our Father"

77-year-old Richard Kantor of Fort Worth, Texas is reporting at this hour that he ain't no gay, and therefore not gonna hold another man's hand during the Our Father.

"I ain't gonna do it. Never did, never will. Wanna hold my hand, ask me on a date; but don't expect nothing less than a whack upside the head with this here stick, you hear me?"

Kantor, who says he typically prefers Latin Mass because there is "no funny business" going on there, said that the last time a man tried holding his hand during the Our Father, he broke two of his fingers. "Turned out to be my son...that one I regret. Still, he shoulda known better than to get all nancy with his old man."

At press time, Kantor was attending a local Novus Ordo, brimming with the anticipation of breaking another couple fingers for the sake of orthodoxy and heterosexuality.

Two Eucharistic Ministers Holding Chalices Vying for You to Drink from Theirs

Eagerly holding out their chalices as you pass by them after receiving communion, two Eucharistic ministers of Holy Communion are reportedly competing to have you drink from theirs.

"Well this lady's closer to me, but that shouldn't necessarily dissuade me from considering drinking from the other one, should it?" you reportedly consider as you realize that you must make a decision one way or the other. "I mean, the first lady offering me her chalice looks like she's doing a pretty sloppy job wiping the rim after people drink from it."

Reports go on to say that, although the second Eucharistic minister is doing a better job wiping the rim of the chalice, she doesn't nearly have as welcoming a face as the first one, but she *was* your CCD teacher years ago. How could you not go to her?

At press time, you've already passed both Eucharistic ministers without drinking from either chalice because you can't remember which of the two the homeless man a dozen or so people in front of you drank from.

Woman at Mass Whispering Words of Consecration in Unison with Priest

An unidentified woman attending Mass at Our Lady of Grace Parish today found it necessary to audibly mumble all the words of the consecration in unison with the priest, sources are confirming.

"Take this, all of you, and eat of it: for this is my body which will be given up for you," the middle-aged woman mumbled, raising her hands in the air to help the presiding priest transubstantiate the Body and Blood.

"Take this, all of you, and drink from it: for this is the chalice of my blood, the blood of the new and eternal covenant, which will be poured out for you and for many for the forgiveness of sins," she then whispered just low enough to be respectful, but loud enough for everyone to recognize how often she frequents Mass. "Do this in memory of me."

At press time, the woman had turned to thank everyone for coming to Mass, and had moved near a child to bless him with her self-consecrated hands.

Priest Tells Lighthearted Story to Begin Homily about Eternal Damnation

23-year-old St. Agatha Parish parishioner Thomas Rudolph confirmed Sunday that all the funny stories the priest was telling during the homily meant that he was about to preach about damnation.

"The silly, lighthearted stories he tells are his way of reminding people that a homily about damnation doesn't have to be all gloom and doom," said Rudolph, bracing himself for the awkward transition. "Last time he talked about damnation, his transition was about how lately, people had been talking about the apocalypse like there was no tomorrow. Yeah, it was bad."

"And, naturally, I asked her what had happened to her crops," Fr. Gregory Anderson told his parishioners as he came to the conclusion of his lighthearted story. "I told her... 'Ma'am, I know a little about armageddon, but it looks like you're having an issue with...farmageddon.' Speaking of armageddon, let us remember that our Lord came not to condemn but to save."

Rudolph told EOTT that as "obnoxious and passive-aggressive" as Fr. Anderson's method was, it definitely worked.

"When I say it works, I mean that sincerely. He spends close to thirteen, fourteen minutes on his story, then says something like, 'Listen, go to confession or you're probably going to hell,' then walks away from the pulpit, wipes sweat from his brow, and begins the Profession of Faith. It's actually kinda genius now that I think of it."

Folk Mass Band Upset over Masses Interrupting Their Concerts

Lead guitarist at St. Therese Parish in Yonkers, New York, Blake Jennings, is outraged over what he calls "years of concerts being interrupted by the Mass."

The 56-year-old accountant and father of three has played with his band at the 9:30 Folk Mass since 2009. "Our fans love us," Jennings said after Sunday Mass. "You can see it in their eyes...the way they droop down, lazily closing as we play...as if they're entering into some kind of ecstasy. Or the way some in the parish are so moved they just can't stand another moment of joy, and simply walk out...presumably to get some air."

But according to Jennings, many in the band have been becoming ever frustrated with the frequent interruptions to their concerts. "Father's always interrupting...always trying to upstage us. First it's a gospel, then a homily, eventually the words of consecration... There's always something with this guy."

Jennings has recently begun a petition, and hopes to get 2,000 signatures to send to the diocese.

Friend's Excuses for Not Making It to Mass Getting Pretty Elaborate

After having skipped Mass for eleven out of the past thirteen Sundays, local Catholic Michael Fremont's excuses for why he has skipped Mass have become more and more elaborate, sources are confirming.

Fremont, who reportedly says he would go to Mass every day if time and circumstances permitted, has now begun to offer concerned Catholic friends extravagant stories filled with intricate details about why he had to miss Mass.

"Michael used to just say that he had slept in," said longtime friend Paula Redlitz. "But once he had used that excuse a few times, he began coming up with new ones every Sunday. First it started with his car not starting. Then he said that he had to deliver a baby in the middle of gridlock traffic. One time he said that his dog ate his Bible. I called him out on this one saying that we're not Protestants and don't bring our Bibles to Mass. I remember he just said, 'Oh, yeah…I meant my missal…. My dog ate my missal.'"

Other friends of Fremont say that at first the excuses were frustrating, but that after getting used to them, they had to admit that they were actually becoming pretty impressive. "We all had to admit that he was really talented," said Robert Koker, a childhood friend of Fremont. "One time he said that he had gotten up on time for Mass, but realized that he had no clue what happened the night before and that he had had a massive headache. He told me that he forgot where his car was. He was also wondering why he had a tattoo on his face and why there was a tiger in his hotel bathroom."

Koker went on to report that he had once seen three large stacks of what looked like third or fourth drafts of excuses sitting on Fremont's desk at home. "It was amazing. There were all these details like times and people's names and descriptions of things like the weather and temperature. He had all these fabricated details he wanted to memorize so that no one would ever catch him in his lies. Even his walls were covered with images of people and places with red strings connecting different pictures like the walls of a serial killer. One of the stories I saw before he walked in on me had an image of himself dressed like Rambo, and he was riding a unicorn over a rainbow as he shot members of ISIS with a machine gun. I can't wait to hear that one."

Rude, Ungrateful Nine-Month-Old Crying
All throughout Mass

In one of the most childish and ungrateful spectacles ever witnessed in St. Margaret Parish, nine-month-old Isabella Stone cried hysterically throughout Sunday morning Mass, blatantly disregarding Christ's sacrifice on the cross for her, sources are reporting.

Little Isabella, who has had a nine-month track record of not appreciating *anything* that Christ has done for her, and who clearly does not act as one who has been redeemed by the blood of the Lamb, wept all throughout Mass like some spoiled little princess, too caught up in her own selfish desires to be fed and changed than to sit quiet and still out of respect for the Lord.

"I don't know where we went wrong," said Isabella's mother as she wept beside her husband. "We knew we had screwed up with this one on the day she was baptized. All she did was cry and cry as if she didn't care that she was becoming a Catholic. In fact, it was almost as if she didn't want to be baptized."

St. Margaret pastor Father Reginald Wyman told EOTT that the "ungracious little pagan" had wept as though he were exorcising a demon from her the moment the baptismal water touched her head. "I remember stepping back and thinking, 'Is the holy water burning her skin or something?'"

Witnesses say that the insolent little beast of a child, who remarkably shows not the mark of the beast as foretold in The Book of the Revelation, reportedly wept all the way through

L

the final blessing until she was taken outside, where she immediately stopped crying.

Most Doctrinally Sound Sermon given on the Catholic Faith in past Three Decades Unfortunately given by Protestant Pastor

What some are calling the most mesmerizing, breathtaking, and doctrinally sound sermon delivered on the Catholic Faith in the past three decades, was unfortunately given at the noon service at *Deluge Community Church* in San Marcos, California last Sunday.

"It was so thrilling to learn about what the Catholic Church teaches," said cradle-Catholic Helen Seymour, who accidentally stumbled into the Protestant church service during their one month long *What Other Christians Believe* series. "I go to Mass and listen to the homily every week, so I thought I knew what the Church teaches…things like fellowship, gathering, community, and not judging. But to hear someone teach me that the Church believes in so much more is something I never expected to hear. Who knew there was so much depth to the Faith?"

Seymour, whose biggest fear in life is becoming a Protestant, went on to report that ever since stumbling upon the service, she has decided to skip going to her parish and to begin attending *Deluge* so as not to miss out on the fullness of her Catholic faith.

Search Intensifies for
Missing Reverence during Mass

More than five dozen searchers scoured the Sierra Nevada foothills for the missing reverence at a Mass at the Church of St. Margaret Mary Alacoque yesterday.

Reverence was due to appear promptly for the 9:00 a.m. Mass, but two hours after the Mass had concluded, a search began with helicopters, including a National Guard Blackhawk Helicopter, looking for any signs of reverence.

Using thermal infrared technology, searchers have still not been able to locate any clues to the whereabouts of the reverence expected at Mass, but a spokeswoman for the Church of St. Margaret Mary Alacoque, Dana Whitmore, told EOTT today that several parishioners were being investigated after being seen walking out of Mass wearing shorts and flip flops.

"We cannot release the names of those being questioned at this moment," Whitmore told the press. "But we can say that officials from the diocese have spoken to St. Margaret Mary's pastor, Fr. Neville Mayfield, about why his altar boys and altar girls were allowed to chew gum while staring out into space during the Consecration."

Nine ground search teams made up of the Priestly Fraternity of St. Peter were later dispatched to find reverence. They focused on the areas in and around the pews as well as on the Sanctuary.

Reverence was not the only thing being sought. In another part of the Sierra Nevada foothills, a search was underway near St. Matthew Catholic Church to find solemnity and piety.

Developing: Sick Man Attempting to Shake Your Hand during Sign of Peace

It is being reported this second that the sick man who has been violently, viciously coughing into his hands all Mass has been feverishly trying to get your attention to shake hands during the Sign of Peace.

"I already threw him a peace sign...why does he keep staring?" you ask yourself as you then begin to throw everyone else peace signs so as to have him believe that that's just the way you do it.

The stranger, who has reportedly been wiping his nose of the seemingly perpetual flow of snot running from his reddened nose before conspicuously drying them onto his pants is now leaning forward toward you, smiling and saying, "Peace of Christ," one witness is now reporting.

At press time, you're pretending not to hear him as you lower your kneeler and pretend to busily prepare for the Agnus Dei, mumbling fake prayers under your breath as you do so.

Homily Never Going To End, Sources Confirm

Multiple sources at Prince of Peace Catholic Church in Galveston, Texas have just confirmed that parish pastor Fr. Robert Warner is "never going to wrap up his freaking homily."

29-year-old mother of three Katrin Flores told EOTT that Warner, whose homily was now running more than twenty-five minutes long, did not seem to be losing any steam whatsoever. "There were a couple times there where we thought he was about to shut it down, but then he'd say something like, 'A couple more points I'd like to cover.' But each of those 'points' had sub-points, and then there was that ten-minute span when he went off on a tangent about growing up in Warsaw with his strict-though-not-overbearing mother. Seriously demoralizing."

James Thorpe, who was on his third "restroom break" in just under fifteen minutes, reported that Warner wasn't a terrible speaker, but that he wasn't Fulton Sheen either. "The man's a time vampire," Thorpe said as he suddenly felt an urgent desire to slowly redo his tie before returning to his pew.

At press time, Warner had given the congregation a glimmer of hope by pausing for a few seconds before beginning again with the words, "In 1972...a man by the name of..."

There Was Certainly a Point during My Clown Mass When I Thought, "What the Hell Am I Doing?"

Pastor of St. Genesius Catholic Church in Tuscan, Arizona, Fr. Edmond Harrington, confirmed to reporters this afternoon that at one point during his first Clown Mass, he looked at his oversized checkered shoes and thought to himself, "Edmond Reginold Harrington, what the *hell* are you doing?"

"I mean, don't get me wrong, I don't feel a shred of guilt about it or anything," Harrington told the press as he brushed away a lock of bright red hair from his painted face, "but I mean... who could deny how freaking weird the whole thing was. As a kid I never imagined myself saying a Mass. I also never imagined myself exerting so much time and effort trying to pick up a host off an altar with oversized white gloves. Definitely harder than it looks."

Harrington went on to say that there was another point just moments after he had said the words of consecration and had raised the host when he just paused there a minute, gazing, "not in adoration, but in absolute disbelief" of what the hell he was doing. One deacon said that he knew the Mass was going to be a touch unusual after Harrington handed him a rubber chicken, and asked him to slap him in the face with it some time during the homily. Harrington told EOTT that he had gotten frustrated during the dismissal, after having spent a good minute trying to maneuver his plastic red nose so that he could kiss the altar.

"It was humiliating," he said, before smacking himself in the face with a pie.

5-Year-Old Parishioner Thinks Being Removed from Mass during Homily for Children's Ministry a Complete Load of Bull Crap

Speaking to a group of children gathered in a room next to St. Margret Catholic Church in Beaverton, Oregon this Sunday, 5-year-old parishioner Jacob Kelting expressed his frustration at having to be "herded" out of church and into the Children's Ministry room.

Kelting reported that the idea that children should be removed from the splendor of the Mass just to color in a picture of an awkwardly smiling Jesus standing beside children and a couple sheep was completely "absurd and asinine."

"I don't know…maybe it's just me," Kelting told friends as they wrestled for the lone brown crayon on the table. "Doesn't anyone else think it's condescending to have to get up and walk out like cattle? It's really embarrassing if you ask me."

Kelting's longtime best friend Irvin Conway agreed with Kelting, telling EOTT that it was "indeed ridiculous that some adults could possibly think that children can only learn about the Mass by coloring or constructing banners with a chalice and host beneath their names."

Conway went on to say that the practice was belittling, and suggested that, seeing as how loud and juvenile many of the adults act the moment Mass is over, the pastor of St. Margret Catholic Church, Father John Ruben, ought to consider moving the *parents* out to color and to do other childish activities, and to leave the children to enjoy the loving presence of Christ in the Eucharist.

PARISH LIFE

"Well, we all walked in to church this morning and saw this golden box placed right where our old pastor, Fr. Rick, sat during the Mass," a visibly shaken parishioner, Carli Welk, told reporters. "And we all just looked at each other and were all like, 'What *is* that?' I told everyone to slowly back away from it."

Atheist Friend Promises to Keep Catholic Friend in His Thoughts during Time of Need

Just a day after local Catholic Robert Wilkinson's grandmother passed away, Wilkinson's atheist friend Godfrey Thomas assured his longtime friend that he would indeed keep him in his thoughts.

"Oh, Robert...what can I say? I'm so very sorry for your loss and I assure you that you will be in my thoughts in this sad time," Godfrey reassured Wilkinson as he placed a consoling hand on his shoulder. "I can't imagine the sorrow you're going through right now. I'm sending you good vibes, dear friend. You'll get through this."

Wilkinson also confirmed to mutual friends that along with keeping him in his thoughts and sending him good vibes, he also planned to wish him the best.

A grieving Wilkinson told EOTT this morning that although Thomas and other atheist friends have assured him that they were sending him good and positive energy in this sad time, he really wished he had someone in his life who would just pray for his consolation as well as his grandmother's eternal salvation.

"I really appreciate them keeping me in their thoughts and wishing me the best, but I just can't see how their vibes are going to get my dead grandmother to heaven. Who knows... God works in mysterious ways."

Liturgical Dancer Tests Positive for
Performance-Enhancing Drugs

It is being reported this morning that world-renowned liturgical dancer Doris Griffin has tested positive for performance-enhancing drugs. A USCCB spokesman said that trace amounts of an illegal substance were found in Griffin's blood early Monday morning. This comes just days after reports that Griffin's trainer, Jake Stately, admitted that he had not only injected Griffin before "numerous Masses," but that he also had in his possession one of the syringes used on the 56-year-old dancer.

Griffin, who is best known for her treatise on liturgical dancing, *The Art Of Body Worship, And So Can You,* told EOTT that the drug found in her system may have been the result of an over-the-counter weightloss medicine that she had recently started taking. Meanwhile, friends of Griffin have come to her defense saying that, though she had recently been under a grueling schedule, the liturgical dancing phenomena would never resort to injecting. "The Lord has just blessed her body with such a rhythm...such an ability to properly express the proper flow of worship as to never need any drugs," a friend of Griffin said.

The USCCB Commission for Mass Doping, meanwhile, said that they will be suspending Griffin from participating in all Masses where dancing is involved until they have concluded their investigation. "For the time being, Ms. Griffin will only have access to the Tridentine Low Mass."

Family Fighting for Good Seats at Christmas Mass with the Zeal of 12th Century Crusaders

Reporting that he and his family had been forced from their aisle seat just minutes after acquiring it, 48-year-old Brenden O'Malley told EOTT moments ago that he would "not rest till his aisle seat was once again reclaimed."

"Beset, as I was, and routed from my aisle seat by congregants who only attend the Holy Mass on Christmas and Easter, my family and I surrendered our aisle unwillingly during this the 5th minute of the Christmas vigil," he told EOTT from his seat "smack in the middle of an overly crowded pew." "It all happened so quickly, that we, the zealous ones who come weekly to Holy Mass, were routed by the nominal ones, entering our pews with their bedazzled rosaries around their necks and imperial standards, and both within the church and on the outer banks where many of us were forced to stand for Mass, we cried out in lamentations, 'Save us, O Lord, and reclaim for us those seats that are rightfully ours.'"

Brenden and family went on to say that they, being one of the last of the "devoted ones" were, at that very moment, in constant vigilance so as not to be squeezed in any further by the CE Catholics.

In a desperate letter written to EOTT during a bathroom break, O'Malley wrote,

At first, we were with aisle; comfort and room to move our legs had we. Then, as the nominal ones came minutes after Mass be-

gan, we moved our camp from aisle and proceeded on our journey toward the center of the pew. Five minutes after this, having collected their forces from all sides, again they besieged many of our fellow parishioners, forcing many to stand on the sides, or exiling them to the basement where a secondary, makeshift Mass was erected for the overflow. EOTT, be not fooled by the ushers, those Knights of Columbus, many of whom we have known for years. For, just as we were beginning to be assailed from both outer aisle and center aisle by the latecomers, the usher Hugh and his wife, Lorraine, were riding at the head, leading yet another horde toward our pews. We have been betrayed. But such, it appears, is the will of God. Nevertheless, I ask that you and all whom this letter reaches pray for us and for our brethren in the basement.

Grouchy Catholic Pacified by Son's Goldfish Crackers during Mass

Several witnesses at the Sunday 9:00 a.m. Mass at Our Lady of Fatima parish told EOTT today that a grumpy, pouting man who was "obviously forced to attend Mass by his mean wife," was finally pacified after his son offered him a packet of Goldfish Crackers.

"He was whining the entire time because his wife had taken away his phone," said one witness sitting directly behind the family. "Then he started crawling all over the pew when everyone stood for the Profession of Faith. He was completely out of control."

Another parishioner said she witnessed the cranky husband and father of three begin throwing things at his son before the two got into a fight.

"He was clearly bullying him," the witness said. "I felt for the wife. It's so sad that some people don't have the help they need. Luckily for the rest of us, she finally allowed him some more crackers before grabbing him by the arm and leading him to the cry room where she took him into her lap and put him to sleep."

Several witnesses at the Sunday 9:00 a.m. Mass at Our Lady of Fatima parish told EOTT today that a grumpy, pouting man who was "obviously forced to attend Mass by his mean wife," was finally pacified after his son offered him a packet of Goldfish Crackers.

Drive-Thru Confessions Huge Hit in Local Parish

Reports out of the Church of the Most Holy Trinity in Wichita, Kansas are confirming that last week's launch of their new drive-thru confessional was a complete success.

"It's an absolute blessing," Church Pastor Father Donald Borland told EOTT. "One day I was sitting in the confessional listening to this old man's confessions, and all I could think about was how long this poor old man was standing in line. I remember I thought to my self, 'Self, there's gotta be a better way to do this than to have people standing in line for twenty minutes.'"

So began the idea to create the first drive-thru confessional. "I love it, and it's so simple," Stephanie Randal, a college sophomore said. "You drive up to a menu with a list of all types of sins and combo sins, and you just tell the priest which number or numbers you did on the menu. No chit-chat, no nothing. I remember I told him I committed a number four super-sized, and he asked me to please drive forward. That's it. You drive up to him at the first window, he absolves you, and the last step is you go to the second window where his secretary tells you your total. They call it a penance, I guess...I don't know, I drove right through that part."

Colorado Priest to Appoint Entire Parish Eucharistic Ministers

Saint Perpetua Parish Priest Father Nick Farley announced Friday that he would be appointing every single parishioner at his church an Extraordinary Minister of Holy Communion.

"In due respect to the amount of Extraordinary Ministers needed per Mass, the adage ought to be, the more the merrier," Farley said. Farley later proudly added that all of his current Extraordinary Ministers are so extraordinary that they are not only able to distribute, but to smile as they do so; an aptitude that, Farley believes, is imperative to proper distribution. "We don't want people receiving Jesus from the hands of a somber-looking priest, you know? A happy Jesus should come from the happy hands of a happy minister."

When asked whether appointing an entire congregation of Eucharistic Ministers was excessive, Farley responded, "Absolutely not... Just as each Christian is entrusted an individual Guardian Angel, so then should they be entrusted their own individual Eucharistic Minister."

Skinny Southern California Girl Who Fasted from Carbohydrates and Fatty Foods Not Ready to Give up Her Lenten Fast

Despite having successfully fulfilled her Lenten fast from carbohydrates and fatty foods, skinny SoCal girl Amber Miller announced today that she would be continuing her fast indefinitely out of love for Jesus and her new set of rock-hard abs.

"The Bible says that JC fasted for forty days and forty nights… and that obviously means He fasted from carbohydrates and fatty foods. I wanted to act in imitation of Him," Miller said as she oiled up her arms and stomach for a quick "tan sesh" before she hit up the bar with her girlfriends. "I remember my friends saying, like, Amber, that's so cray, because they know how much I love burritos and stuff, and I was all like, I love Jesus and tight pants so I'm gonna do it. And now I can seriously see myself fasting for my abs, I mean for my Lord, forever. I've never felt so disciplined in my life. Like, ever."

At press time, Miller had announced that she may even consider going to Mass sometime before Christmas.

Spider Finds Unused Piece of Real Estate on Catholic Bible to Build New Web

Cherry Cavatica, daughter of famed animal rights activist and spider Charlotte Cavatica, has found a pristine and unused piece of real estate on which to build her new home, the three month old spider is reporting this morning.

Cavatica found the 6 x 9 inch plot of land just days after having had her home atop a Playstation game console unexpectedly dusted off by its land owner.

"I had finished construction on the web just two days before its destruction," Cavatica told EOTT. "Obviously it was devastating, especially considering that I just recently found out that I'm with egg." Cavatica went on to explain how, after days of searching, her real estate agent informed her about a pristine plot of land on the upper banks of a closet. "I went with her to take a look at the land and was just mesmerized. It was perfect... I remember thinking this the first moment I saw it. The area looked quiet and peaceful. A great place to raise a new family."

Cavatica's real estate agent, Itsy Bitsy, told EOTT that many first-time web owners make the mistake of choosing open spaces to build their homes. "Many spiders find the open space and light very appealing because of all the opportunity to catch flies. While this may be true," Bitsy admits, "the dangers typically far outweigh the benefits." Bitsy recommends spiders choose real estate that is never touched, such as a Catholic Bible. "Many spiders are able to live out their lives on a Catholic

Bible. In fact, generations of spiders could realistically live on a Catholic Bible."

Bitsy gave one more piece of advice for first time web owners: "Not just any Bible will do. The Bible *must* be Catholic and not Protestant. I cannot stress this enough."

Overzealous Priest Overturns the Tables of the Money Changers in Church Gift Shop

In what the police are calling a "fanatical act committed while in the state of a nervous breakdown," Associate Pastor of St. Margaret Catholic Church in Louisville, Kentucky, Father Randy Coelho, walked into the parish gift shop and began to overturn registers as well as tables containing rosaries, scapulars, and other religious goods earlier this morning.

The incident occurred shortly after the conclusion of the 7:00 p.m. Mass, when an "overworked" Coelho appeared to have "snapped" following his first four-Mass day since ordination.

"It was very unusual," said gift shop owner Rosie Culkin. "He's usually so calm. But he came in screaming at us saying, 'Is it not written, my house shall be called a house of prayer? But you have made it into a den of thieves!' So I tried to calm him down and tell him that this was just the gift shop and that the house of prayer was about twenty feet thataway. But he kept flipping everything over, which really sucked cause we have inventory to do tonight."

Culkin went on to say that after also telling [Coelho] that it was not a den of thieves because thieves typically do not come into religious gift shops after Mass ready to purchase religious goods with cash or credit. Coelho told police that he just wanted to make sure they were not selling doves. No charges are expected to be filed.

St. Valentine Makes Impassioned Plea for
Safe Return of Kidnapped Feast Day

In a heart-wrenching moment on the Today Broadcast earlier this morning, 3rd century saint Valentine made an emotional plea to the kidnappers of his feast.

Speaking directly to the camera and with tears in his eyes, St. Valentine begged for the safe return of his beloved feast day, promising that all would be forgiven if it was returned to him safely. "It was definitely emotional," said Today Broadcast host Matt Bauer after the interview. "You could see the pain he's going through. It's been so long since he's experienced the tender embrace of multitudes of Catholic prayers on his feast day."

Bauer went on to express how important it was to keep the abduction in the minds of the general public. Valentine, who lost his feast day some time around the 18th century in England, told Bauer that, "No saint should ever have to feel the loss or abduction of a feast day. I especially feel for saints like St. Patrick, whose feast was abducted by millions of belligerent drunks across the world."

Although the case has been "cold" for some time, Church officials say that they have had some leads, saying that a middle-aged Geoffrey Chaucer had been seen centuries around the abduction associating the day with romantic love.

"We're not saying that Mr. Chaucer is a suspect at this time; only that he may be in connection with the disappearance, and is wanted for questioning," said head investigator Antonio Benini. Valentine has asked the public to stop sending teddy bears, heart-shaped balloons, overpriced flowers, lingerie, and three-hour waits at restaurants, and instead, say a prayer to him.

Report: Man Who's Never Killed Anyone or Anything Like That Doesn't Need to Go to Confession

A new report out today by area Catholic Marcus Dietrich's conscience revealed that the 31-year-old father of two is most certainly *not* in need of the Sacrament of Confession, thanks to never having killed anyone or anything terrible like that.

Data compiled by Dietrich after a moment's reflection upon entering church this morning also showed that he was, indeed, in a proper disposition to receive Communion despite a one-year absence from Mass. "I was so relieved when I found out the results of my study," said an anti-scrupulous Dietrich as he half-knelt, half-rested his bottom on the edge of the pew during the Consecration. "Not that I was really surprised by the results... I mean, sure I don't go to Mass often, or pray, or anything, and I use contraception, but it's not like I go around shooting people in the head or anything psycho like that."

At press time, Dietrich had remembered gravely sinning two days prior after having forgotten to smog his car, consequently allowing fumes to eat away at the ozone layer, leading to global warming, and melting the ice of cute polar bear cubs.

A new report out today by area Catholic Marcus Dietrich's conscience revealed that the 31-year-old father of two is most certainly *not* in need of the Sacrament of Confession, thanks to never having killed anyone or anything terrible like that.

Pastor Encourages Parishioners to Use New Click-To-Confess Feature on Church Website

After revealing new updates to the parish website, pastor of St. Claire Church, Fr. Nicholas Walker, told his flock that should they have to confess, to henceforth do so by the new "Click-to-Confess" feature on the parish website.

"I began to notice a rise in parishioners desiring confessions, but I couldn't get to all of them with the fifteen minutes I have allotted for confessions a week," Walker said. The Click-to-Confess feature allows penitents to confess anonymously from the comforts of home or a coffee shop. "They simply log on, click from the long list of sins available to confess, and send. They'll receive an automated response within five to ten minutes with an electronic receipt of their confession, as well as confirmation of their absolution and recommended penance."

"It's really an amazing new feature," one parishioner told EOTT. "One confession I had last week was really awkward and embarrassing so I simply clicked the 'Mumble' button. I got a response back a few minutes later asking, 'What's that?' I clicked the 'Mumble' button again and received an absolution about two minutes later."

Parishioners Mystified by Sudden Appearance of Mysterious, Shiny Golden Box

Just weeks after being appointed a new young pastor, parishioners at St. Agatha Catholic Church in Houston, Texas were baffled this morning when they saw a large, gold, "magical box-looking thingy" sitting directly behind the altar as they entered St. Agatha Catholic Church.

"Well, we all walked in to church this morning and saw this golden box placed right where our old pastor, Fr. Rick, sat during the Mass," a visibly shaken parishioner Carli Welk told reporters. "And we all just looked at each other and were all like, 'What *is* that?' I told everyone to slowly back away from it."

Welk is now being heralded as a hero after calmly rushing all of the parishioners outside where she proceeded to dial 9-1-1. "I don't consider myself a hero," she later reported to a local Houston area news affiliate. "I just did what I had to, you know? We didn't know what was in there or whether the thing itself was dangerous. Some thought it was just an ornate refrigerator carrying some kind of supernatural bread... Others actually thought there might actually be a body in there. Better safe than sorry."

At press time, state officials had been called to the scene after St. Agatha's new pastor was seen on his knees before the shiny gold box, reportedly transfixed and completely succumbing to the powers of the box, which are yet to be identified.

Not Enough Banners in Churches Lately Biggest Problem Facing Catholic Church

A new survey out this week shows that American Catholics see the diminishing number of banners inside their churches as the biggest problem facing the Catholic Church.

A survey from the Pew Forum on Religion and Public Life asked U.S. Catholics to describe the problems facing the Church, and found that 47% thought the most important issue was the diminishing number of banners inside their churches. The second most pressing issue for U.S. Catholics was in regards to the final few Holy Days of Obligation left on the liturgical calendar, and having those obligations altogether and perpetually dispensed.

"The results are very fascinating, yet not so shocking," Pew Forum on Religion and Public Life President Patricia Contratto told EOTT. "We know how well purple banners with cute little sheep help parishioners reflect on the bloody, gruesome death of our Lord during Lent. And we've seen some pastors in recent years begin to decrease the number of banners in their churches, and I think that the average U.S. Catholic is voicing their concern. They're telling their Bishops and Cardinals what they want to see in their churches. They're not looking for an encyclical to help them meditate on the Lord. All they want are images of a sheep and fish on purple banners to help them remember Jesus during the Lenten season."

Man Who's Able to Bring Christ down from Heaven to Earth Required to Get Permission from Parish Council for Something

Fr. Kenneth Roberts of The Holy Spirit Catholic Church in Albany, New York announced today that despite having the power and authority to bring Christ down from Heaven during the Mass, he is still, for some unfathomable reason, required to get permission from the Parish Council about most everything he does.

"I guess I'm just kinda confused," Roberts told EOTT after his request for money to purchase a more proper tabernacle was denied. "I'll give them the benefit of the doubt though... Sometimes people forget that I'm able to do things that angels can't even do."

Parish Council member Joan Merriman told EOTT that, although she was sorry about their decision in this particular case, she could not apologize for his requirement to pass things by them before making decisions. "Although Fr. Roberts does indeed act in persona Christi as he forgives me of all my deepest, darkest sins, it's still necessary for him to go through us so that he doesn't make any silly decisions like spending money on traditional vestments when we could be using that money on new banners and balloons for the church."

Report: Woman Cannot Seriously Still Be in Confessional

While patiently waiting in line for confessions earlier this afternoon, parishioners of St. Jude parish in Long Island, New York were questioning whether or not someone had actually entered the confessional at all.

After waiting some fifteen minutes, frustrated parishioner Betty Swaim told EOTT that she could have sworn that she heard laughter coming from the confessional. "Oh, yeah, go ahead... laugh it up... It's not like anyone else here needs to confess."

Another parishioner, Scott Chaney, confirmed that a woman did indeed enter, as he simultaneously questioned himself as to whether the mysterious woman may have actually already exited the confessional without anyone paying attention. "No, I did...didn't I see her enter? Yeah, I did see her enter. Like twenty minutes ago."

45-year-old Jane Browning, who was third in line when confessions began, and nearing the end of a rosary she never thought she would actually get through, told EOTT that she was baffled as to how someone could take so long. "Look, I'm not trying to say anything... I mean, good for her, you know? But if she's seriously just in there laughing and having a good ol' time while we stand out here like idiots, I swear I'll bust open that door and drag her out."

At press time, Chaney was awkwardly approaching the confessional door just to be sure.

Study: Every Large Catholic Family in the U.S. Has A "Bernadette"

A new study out today has found that every Catholic family of seven or more children had at least one girl named "Bernadette." The study put out by the United States Conference of Catholic Bishops asked the eighty-five large Catholic families left in the United States for a list of their children's names, and found that all eighty-five families had at least one "Bernadette."

"Along with one 'Bernadette,' one in three families had a 'Therese,' and two in three had a 'John Paul,'" the head of the study, Monsignor Benjamin Clark, told EOTT. The study also found that of Catholic families with nine or more children, two in three had at least one child who wore a jean jumper that reached their feet, and a long-sleeved white shirt beneath it. "We also found an alarming trend that, with the popularity of 'Bernadette' in large Catholic families, many of these families were also beginning to name their children names such as 'Soubirous' and other awkward last names of saints such as 'Pio.' We predict that we will have our first 'Of Lisieux,' or 'Pius X' within the next ten years."

Clark went on to say that with the help of General Motors, they were able to find that 87% of large white vans sold in the U.S. were sold to these families. The other 13% were sold to people trafficking large quantities of cocaine across the U.S.-Mexico border.

Priest Accidentally Leaves Lapel Mic on in Confessional; Your Darkest, Deepest Secrets Revealed to Everyone

It was reported today that your parish pastor, Father John Frank, accidently left his lapel mic on after having finished saying Mass, consequently revealing to everyone in the church all of your deepest and darkest secrets. The news came just moments after revealing for the first time that thing you did during the summer of '98, and all the people who suffered as a consequence of your shameless acts.

"I couldn't believe what I was hearing," said the woman who was behind you in confession, and who had actually let you go first so she could finish examining her conscience. "I almost fainted when I heard what was coming out of that confessional. I thought to myself, 'What kind of person is this?'" The woman went on to explain how she had tried to open the door, but that for some reason it was locked.

The third person in line behind you told EOTT that they tried their best to knock on the door while you confessed those things you did in Vegas the weekend prior, but to no avail. "You wouldn't answer the door for some reason. We all just had to stand there and listen to your litany of sins as you nervously confessed one sin after another after another."

Other witnesses reported that they had not in all their lives ever committed even one of those sins, and that they could not believe that you of all people could and would actually commit all of those sins all by yourself. Presently, word is spreading like wildfire about what you confessed, and everyone cannot help but to see you in a different light, including your mother, and everyone who has ever loved you.

On Good Friday, Christians to Celebrate the Holy Feast of the Fastest and Most Violent Reversal of Public Opinion in History

With Passion Week beginning today, Catholics and non-Catholic Christians from across the globe gather to contemplate the events leading up to the Holy Feast of the Fastest and Most Violent Reversal of Public Opinion in History.

Passion Week begins with Palm Sunday, which commemorates Jesus' triumphant entry into Jerusalem, and the crowd's acceptance of him as "Hosanna." Millions of Christians worldwide will honor the day by carrying palm leaves in processions to recall Jesus riding a donkey into Jerusalem, when cheering crowds waved palms, hailing what they expected to be a political savior. Then on Friday, Christians will honor the day by someway or another denying Christ by either word or deed, to recall the Feast of the Fastest and Most Violent Reversal of Public Opinion in History, when those same people who had accepted Jesus as King of Israel just days prior, inexplicably, spontaneously, and quite violently changed their minds and demanded that he be crucified.

Founder of *Splendor of Truth Ministries,* Nicholas Lebish, recently explained to EOTT why Good Friday is such an important day for Christians, saying that it is a day to contemplate the "complete absurdity and feebleness of the human mind."

"We mourn on that day for two deaths. First, we mourn the

condemnation and death of Christ, and second, we mourn for the death of common sense," Lebish said, moments after meditating on what he considered should be a sixth mystery in the Sorrowful Mysteries. "If this isn't a mystery in the literal sense, then I have no idea what is. You have the mysteries of The Agony, The Scourging, Crowing, Carrying, and Crucifixion, but what is missing is the inexplicable and unprecedented mystery of such a rapid, spontaneous and quite vicious change of public opinion that allowed for Jesus' torture and murder."

Protestant Friend Knows All He Needs to Know about Catholic Church

Area Protestant Ezekial Atkinson reported earlier this morning that he did not need a lecture on Church teaching because he "already knows everything he needs to know about the Catholic Church."

The stunning revelation came just moments after longtime Catholic friend Gerald Prescott asked Atkinson whether he ever considered that [Atkinson] might not actually hate the Church as much as he thinks, but rather, in the words of Fulton Sheen, "hate what he wrongly considers to be the Church."

Atkinson, a youth pastor at East Bay United Pentecostal, told Prescott that he grew up a Catholic, and even used to be an altar boy. "I went to Catholic school, Gerald...I know what the Church teaches," Atkinson reportedly said. "If you guys ever picked up a Bible you'd know what it means when Paul says, 'And grieve not the Holy Spirit of God, whereby ye are sealed unto the day of redemption.' So don't talk to me about going to confession with a priest. I've been sealed with the blood of the Lamb, so nothing can separate me from the love of God. And don't even get me started on Mary."

"I went to Catholic school, Gerald...I know what the Church teaches," Atkinson reportedly said. "If you guys ever picked up a Bible you'd know what it means when Paul says, 'And grieve not the Holy Spirit of God, whereby ye are sealed unto the day of redemption.' So don't talk to me about going to confession with a priest. I've been sealed with the blood of the Lamb, so nothing can separate me from the love of God. And don't even get me started on Mary."

Parishioner at the Back of Long
Confession Line Sure Is Optimistic

Walking to the back of a nauseatingly long confession line with only five minutes to go before Mass yesterday evening, an undeterred and naively optimistic Christopher Repin smiled and greeted penitents in front of him.

"God bless you guys," a cheerful and relaxed Repin told people around him as he held up two fingers in a peace sign for those near the front of the line. Sources say that Repin appeared so at ease in spite of his terrible chances of actually making it in, that many parishioners, who were repeatedly and frantically checking their watches, just assumed he was "nuts," and tried to avoid making eye contact with the confident freak.

31-year-old Bill Weber, who was second in line, told EOTT that he initially chuckled to himself when he saw Repin actually get in line. "I looked at my watch then looked at the line and I was like *please*. I'm second up and I'm just barely gonna make it. But the guy's so cheerful and positive...as if he actually has a chance. Guy must be a wacko."

At press time, parishioners in line were relieved to see Repin glance at his watch.

Every Holy Day of Obligation on Liturgical Calendar Deferred to Easter

A spokesman for the United States Conference of Catholic Bishops announced today that beginning on the Feast of the Ascension of the Lord, every holy day of obligation listed on the Liturgical Calendar, including Sundays, would from here on be deferred to Easter.

The announcement came as welcome news to many Catholics who found the near-impossible obligations imposed on them by their bishops simply too difficult to fulfill. Spokeswoman for the USCCB, Sister Maxine Howard, told the press this morning that the removal of nearly every obligatory holyday was a long time coming.

"This will most certainly come as a relief to many Catholics who were falling into sin because of unfeasible Church requirements."

One Catholic we spoke to outside the Church of St. Mark said that he agreed with the decision, and was relieved to know that he would no longer have to sacrifice any more of his time. "It's not that I don't like going to church... It's just that I don't like going to church days after I just *went*. And to think that from now on I'll only be obliged to go once a year? It's just too kind of our bishops. They're always looking out to make sure we don't over-burden ourselves."

Vacationing Catholic Excited to See What Liturgical Abuses Practiced in Visiting Parish

Returning to his hometown with his family for the first time in over five years, Catholic family man Alex Trumble voiced his desire Saturday afternoon to try out a new parish where he and his family could "get a taste of the local liturgical abuses practiced this side of the country."

"We've been in Folk Masses and Clown Masses back home, but I hear they have an interesting Muslim-themed Mass over here," Trumble said of the rumors he has read online. "That's an abuse I think my family will never forget. And I guess that's the point. I'm trying to give my family a vacation they'll never forget.

"The Church is fashioned like a mosque on the inside and everyone brings their own prayer rugs and they kneel and stand and do all the Islamic gestures while Mass is said. Sounds like it'll be unforgettable."

Trumble went on to say that he knows how important having memorable vacations are, remembering the time when he was a child in the 60s and experiencing his first Novus Ordo.

"Oh, it wasn't liturgical abuse or anything, but to me and my family at the time... It's just something that never left me. I remember my father telling me that we had just witnessed our first ever not-as-good-as-Tridentine-Mass Mass. Ah, the memories."

Catholic School Children Offended by
Dumbed Down Homily

Students at St. Therese of Carmel Academy walked out of Mass confounded earlier this morning after parish priest Fr. Ted Cordova delivered an over simplified homily about the Lord's command to forgive "not seven but seventy-seven times."

"My mind's still totally blown away with how stupid Fr. Ted thinks we are," eighth-grader Mary Brueland told EOTT as she tried to make sense of the homily. "Honestly, I'm more confused about the Bible now than I ever was." Brueland went on to painfully describe the homily, saying that Cordova spoke real slow and condescendingly as he paced up and down the aisle "like a Protestant pastor."

"And he told us how even though Christ said to forgive seventy-seven times, that he didn't literally mean 'seventy-seven.' Then he explained what 'literally' means. And then he told us how 'seventy-seven' was just a symbol, and that a symbol is something that represents something else. In this case 'seventy-seven' represents perfection, and that perfection means being like Jesus, who loves us all very, very, very much. I'm actually not even sure how he got back to the main point of God's mercy... I got lost when he started giving us the definition of 'very, very, very much.' I mean...he does know we're kids and not idiots, right?"

Liberal Catholic University to Replace Church with Massive Cafeteria

To help accommodate the diverse palates of Mater Dei University's large Catholic student-body, President Jon Heinz has announced plans to build the largest cafeteria in the U.S.

The cafeteria would eventually replace the university's main church at the center of campus. The plan was announced in a letter to donors Friday requesting extra funds to help pay for the multi-million dollar project.

"Our students, like Catholic students all around the country, like nice, big cafeterias. They're cafeteria Catholics, if you will. And here they'll have all the freedom to pick and choose from a vast array of foods."

When asked what types of food the cafeteria planned to serve, Heinz said that the menu would never be set in stone, but rather, would be "ever evolving...like the ever evolving tastes of our students. Many of our students these days are so bogged down with their own parties and events that they often don't have time to sit down and wait as warm meals are prepared for them. Therefore, we're considering having a large selection of foods that won't take time to heat up—lukewarm foods that are neither hot nor cold."

Father Teaches Son How to Love Jesus without Having to Commit Whole Life to Him

Explaining how imparting a faith in Jesus Christ in his son without having him become an awkward religious "zealot" is his primary goal, a local Catholic father told EOTT this morning that teaching his son the importance of going to Mass on Christmas and Easter was enough to go to heaven.

"Ben is hitting that age when he's trying to find out who he is," said father of Ben, Douglas Jackson, noticing recent changes in his son. "Lately he's been going to Mass every day with his mother, and has shown some interest in becoming an altar boy. It's my duty as his father to teach him many things like not doing drugs, and not fully committing your life to Christ."

Douglas Jackson went on to say that committing one's life to Christ is a perilous road fraught with chastity, begging for money for the Church, chastity, having your father have to explain to his buddies why his son became a priest, and chastity as well.

"Loving Jesus is important to me, don't get me wrong. You have to love Jesus to get to heaven, but there are ways to do this without having to neglect your duties as a son to provide his father with a grandson and heir to the pool cleaning business I've built."

Diocese of Gaylord, Michigan to Change Its Name to Peoplewhostrugglewithsamesexattractionlord, Michigan

Parishioners in the Diocese of Gaylord, Michigan are being asked by their new Bishop, Steven Raica, to begin referring to themselves as Peoplewhostrugglewithsamesexattractionlordians.

The news came just days after Raica was installed as Bishop of the flamboyant Roman Diocese. Raica told parishioners during his first homily as Bishop that, basing his decision on Sacred Scripture, all Catholics residing in Gaylord should not act upon their citizenship, and henceforth avoid the term Gaylord.

"I don't care whether you believe that you were born in Gaylord, or whether you simply woke up one day to find yourself living here. We are more than mere citizens of this city... We are children of God, who calls us to fulfill His will and to unite to the sacrifice of the Lord's cross the difficulties we may encounter from being from this region of the country."

Raica went on to say that, although acting upon their citizenship by means of voting or running for office in the city is contrary to natural law and therefore cannot be approved, he assured Catholics living in the diocese that they can still serve a purpose.

In the end, Raica said that being from Gaylord ultimately does not satisfy the desires of the heart. "I've heard from many a family member of those living here, asking if I could help their loved ones move back home. But this is not a simple fix. As the saying goes, 'You can take the man out of Gaylord, but you can't take the Gaylord out of the man.'"

At press time, former Major League Baseball player Those-withhomosexualtendencies Perry has come out in favor of the proposed name change.

Local Catholic Man to Live Life How He Wants; Only God Can Judge Him

Local lapsed Catholic Jonathan Winters confirmed this morning that he was going to live his life the way he wanted, going on to confirm that only God could judge him, regardless of whatever anyone thought of his lifestyle.

According to sources close to the 28-year-old, Winters planned to continue his life of lust and excess without the slightest regard for what anyone thought of him because ain't nobody know him but God.

"Ain't nobody know me," Winters told EOTT, as he fired one up. "Ain't nobody in the world know me and my soul but God. It says it right there in the Bible too. Only God can judge me."

When asked what he meant by only "God could judge" him, Winters said that it was in the Bible that only God could judge him and nobody else, though he could not locate it in the Bible because the only time he ever actually held one was when he swore on the Bible that Marley was the man.

New Orlando Parish to Be Named
"Our Lady of Good Intentions"

After months of debate, officials have confirmed that a new Catholic church slated to be built this summer has officially been named *Our Lady of Good Intentions*.

The name of the multi-million dollar church designed by Florida priest Fr. William Kessler has been debated for the past two years. But after a poll was taken by Orlando residents last month between *Our Lady of Good Intentions* and *Our Lady of Those Who Mean Well*, the former title narrowly won out with 54% of the vote.

"Both names would've certainly worked," Kessler said as he peered out onto the vacant lot where thousands of Catholics will soon be taught that all Jesus desires is a person who means well. "In fact, one of the early front runners for me personally was *Our Lady of Those Who, Even Though They Might Not Attend Mass Regularly, at Least, You Know, Have Good Hearts and Try to Be Good Because God Is in Your Heart, Anyway, so Don't Judge Me, Because God Said Not to Judge*."

Kessler went on to quote Shakespeare's famous play *Romeo and Juliet*, saying, "That which we call a rose by any other name would smell as sweet," and that no matter the name, the point is that people feel welcome, and don't feel like they're being judged; as long as they're good people who mean well.

At press time, Kessler had declined to comment on what constitutes "good."

OCD Parishioner Making Sure All Missals Upright

With Mass just two hours away, sources confirmed that OCD parishioner Michael Kenneth has spent the past ten minutes moving from pew to pew making sure all of the missals are upright and perfectly spaced from one another.

"I seriously don't understand how anyone could be so careless as to how they return the missals and music hymnals," Kenneth reported as he frantically made sure that each music hymnal was perfectly aligned behind a missal. "There's really space for four missals to sit side by side, but that really cramps everything. The best thing to do is to have three side by side with just about an inch of spacing between each."

After properly ordering the missals and hymnals, Kenneth reportedly began to order the donation envelopes as he continually glared at other parishioners who mind-bogglingly chose to spend their time in prayer rather than "man up" and assist the growingly discontented OCD parishioner.

"It just kinda blows my mind. You use the hymnal and put it back the way you got it. Why would anyone choose to flip it backwards and upside down before returning it? I'm convinced it's gotta be some anti-Catholic liberal nutcase. Christianity is indeed that last acceptable prejudice."

" **I**t just kinda blows my mind. You use the hymnal and put it back the way you got it. Why would anyone choose to flip it backwards and upside down before returning it? I'm convinced it's gotta be some anti-Catholic liberal nutcase. Christianity is indeed that last acceptable prejudice. "

Study: Majority of Instances of Protestants Praying for Friends Involves Becoming Mediator between Man and God

According to a study commissioned by the National Committee of Catholic Apologists (NCCA) published today, 100% of Protestants praying for friends and loved ones involves the process of kinda sorta becoming mediators between God and said friends and loved ones.

"Although Protestants typically believe that Jesus is the sole mediator between God and man, and that praying to the saints goes against scripture, which states that there is only one mediator and that that mediator is Jesus Christ, our study shows that 100% of Protestants who participated in our study had absolutely no clue that praying on someone's behalf is nearly the definition of becoming a mediator, although not the same as Christ, obviously."

The NCCA went on to reveal that, although those Protestants studied mentioned reservations about praying to dead people, all saints interviewed for the study mentioned that, due to their proximity to God compared to those Protestants who partook in the study, they were more alive than anyone.

Unbelievably Wealthy Parishioner Has
Some Great Fundraising Ideas

Edward Goodman, parishioner and parish council member at Our Lady of Grace in Tampa Bay, Florida, has some great ideas for fundraising, he is reporting. The parish is in need of a new air-conditioning system as well as a roof repair, according to the pastor, Fr. Greg Nussbaum, whose total lifetime income will be a fraction of what Goodman makes in a year.

"I think we should definitely start the process by sending out a flyer to all parishioners explaining the problem with the roof," Goodman said to the rest of the parish council. "I don't think we need to explain the broken air conditioner. You can't really miss that lately!"

"Then," Goodman continued, as he reflected on the eight apartment buildings he owns as well as the Bentley he drove to church in, "we can ask each family in the parish to donate ten dollars. If they all donate, that'll be enough to cover the air conditioner. I'll be the first to donate to kick things off," he said as he signed a check for exactly ten dollars.

The parish council continued to listen as Goodman unfolded his master plan. "We need a bake sale. Not one of those chintzy little ones they do over at St. Anastasia's. I'm talking big time. We can use the church hall free of charge, and take out an ad in the Pennysaver to spread the word."

As the parish council considered the bake sale idea proposed by the man who had just finished telling them about the Euro trip he took with his family for three weeks, and who had paid more in taxes last year than the rest of the parish council made in income combined, Goodman sat back, pondering the amount of grace he was receiving that very moment for the guidance he was providing the council free of charge.

The funds made by the bake sale would be increased, according to Goodman, by a car auction. "We get ourselves a Camry, and if we sell one thousand tickets at one hundred dollars apiece, that'll cover the initial cost of the car and make us more than enough to fix the roof," Goodman continued, apparently believing $100 to be a reasonable amount to charge for a raffle ticket, and seemingly unconscious of the fact that he basically made the amount needed for the roof and air-conditioning through stocks in the time it took him to explain his idea. "Heck," he continued, "I'd buy a couple tickets myself maybe, just to show support."

After their meeting, the parish council members spent some time chatting in the parking lot while Fr. Greg thanked Goodman for his great ideas and valuable contribution, which came in the form of warm carbon dioxide molecules issuing from his trachea.

At press time, Goodman was waving to the rest of the parish council from his Bentley as he drove away, his window down slightly, just a tiny bit, about the width of the eye of a needle.

S.C. NAOUM

After Twenty-Six Weeks of Anticipation, Twenty-Seventh Sunday in Ordinary Time Just around Corner

After twenty-six weeks of eager anticipation, it was reported today that hundreds of millions of Catholics from across the Christian West began preparations for this week's long-awaited celebration of the twenty-seventh Sunday in Ordinary Time.

"Really, outside of Christmas and Easter...and the feasts of the Assumption, Ascension, All Saint's Day, Immaculate Conception, Ash Wednesday, Palm Sunday, Holy Thursday, and Good Friday, there's really not a more exciting Sunday for a Catholic," creator of the popular *Catholicism* series, Father Robert Barron, told EOTT.

"Well, then you have the Sundays in the Christmas and Easter Season, and the minor feast days, but after that, it's all about the twenty-seventh Sunday in Ordinary Time. Sorry, I forgot about Holy Saturday, Divine Mercy Sunday, Trinity Sunday, Pentecost Sunday..."

Barron went on to announce that he planned on producing a new twelve-part DVD series about the twenty-seventh week in Ordinary Time titled *Ordinary*.

At press time, leaders of the militant group Al-Shabaab said that they would cease all attacks on Christian groups in the Middle East and elsewhere out of respect for "Christians around the world who hold dear, the twenty-seventh Sunday in Ordinary Time."

VOCATIONS

"Father Vincent exemplifies the complete opposite of what fashion is meant to be. He continues to wear white months after Labor Day."

"One Pastor for 3,000 Families? Yeah, That Sounds about Right," Pastor Reports

Local pastor and one of only two priests serving the close to 3,000-family-strong parish of St. Claire Catholic Church reported this morning that the number of parishioners that he and his fellow priest had to serve was perfectly normal and acceptable.

"Oh yeah, this is *perfectly* normal and *exactly* as it should be," said a twitching Pastor Kevin Jefferson as he simultaneously puffed on three cigarettes. "I've just spent the past two years in a row saying Mass, hearing confessions, baptizing, confirming and so on, and I'm really hoping to get a day off next week... yeah, that'd be nice. Oh yeah, real nice... I don't even need a day... How about half a day...half a day? Haha. Did I say half a day? Crazy me, how about an hour...just an hour. FOR THE LOVE OF GOD, AN HOUR! HALF HOUR...OK, FIFTEEN MINUTES, SOMETHING...ANYTHING!"

At press time—"HOW ABOUT FIVE MINUTES? I'M BEGGING YOU! I NEED TO USE THE RESTROOM! Oh, crap... too late. OK fine. And what are your sins, my son?"

Dominican Still Wearing White
Months after Labor Day

Mr. Blackwell's annual worst dressed list came out yesterday, naming popular Dominican radio personality Father Vincent Serpa as Worst Dressed Celebrity of 2012. "Father Vincent exemplifies the complete opposite of what fashion is meant to be," Cherry Dean, a Blackwell representative, told the press after the announcement yesterday morning.

"In lieu of Diesel, he wears Habit; for coat he dons cape; in spite of the established framework of fashion, he continues to wear white months after Labor Day."

It is the first time in the fifty-three-year history of Blackwell's Worst Dressed that a Dominican radio personality took home the award. When asked what he thought of being named Worst Dressed, Serpa responded, "Thank you."

Dissident Legionary Parts Hair in Middle

Speaking to an assembly of Legionary of Christ seminarians this week, Communications Director for the Legionaries, Jim Fair, expressed outrage over the most recent scandal to hit the fragile religious congregation when just last week Legionary priest Ronald McKellen was caught on tape with his hair parted down the middle; a clear violation of the rules and regulations of the congregation.

"It is an outrage! It is a scandal, scandal, scandal!" Fair screamed to reporters gathered late yesterday evening. "Is it a sign of the times...I can't say. Is it a sign of the end...I dare not say."

It was just recently that the congregation was forced to acknowledge that its founder, Marcial Maciel, had fathered children in spite of his vow of celibacy.

"The Maciel thing was one thing," one seminarian said, with tears in his eyes, "but this...this is too much."

Man Who Must Be Some Sort of Masochist or Mutant Chooses to Wear Collar, Never Have Sex

In a case baffling his family and friends, sources have confirmed this morning that 23-year-old Donny Reynolds, who is clearly masochistic, has decided to devote his life to Christ and to never have sex, although there are other ways to devote your life to Christ without giving up having a wife and children.

"There were signs and we missed them," Reynolds' mother, Donna Reynolds, told EOTT in an emotional interview. "A couple years ago he began attending daily Mass although we're only obligated to attend on Sundays. Then we noticed him reading the Bible although we're not Protestant. I don't know... I blame myself."

"It's really one of the weirdest cases I have ever come across," said psychologist Dr. Edward Benton. "He seems perfectly normal in all other aspects of his life, except for this one exception of desiring a life of poverty and chastity."

Benton went on to say that he hoped that with medication and time, Reynolds would begin to see signs of improvement, and perhaps even his desire to one day get married and have sex and be like everyone else would return.

Android Priests Being Developed to Help Say Mass, Hear Confessions

The Vatican has confirmed reports today that an agreement has been reached with the International Federation of Robotics (IFR) to begin development of what they are calling "Clergy-droids."

The news comes as a relief to many seminary directors around the world who have seen their numbers plummet in the past few decades. "With so few priests and so many Catholics, this is going to help assure that every parish not only has a pastor of their own, but also an associate pastor," Father Tobi Riland told the press earlier this morning. "I have had the pleasure of having a prototype absolve me of my sins. I'll tell you one thing... he didn't...excuse me, *it* didn't forget the words of absolution!"

One Vatican official, Monsignor Phillip Rudolph, who spearheaded the negotiations, told EOTT that, "when you see those big, blue glowing eyes peering through the confessional grill at you, it feels as though they're burning right through you. Seriously though, they freaking burn. Look at this burn mark on my throat. It's a malfunction in the prototype that the IFR promises to resolve before their final launch next May."

Another issue with the clergydroid prototype Fr. SRT4-11392 includes a recent frying of some of its mechanisms and kinematics after an altar boy attempted to pour water on the clergydroid's titanium fingers. Witnesses say that Fr. SRT4-11392's final words before catching fire were, "Lord, wash away my iniqui...iniqui...iniqui...iniqui. Oh, no...just when I was learning to love."

Maestro Who Conducts Symphony with Back Facing Audience Labeled Radical Traditional

After conducting his first symphony since being named Maestro of the New Mexico Philharmonic, Chinese-born Li Wei Chen has been under heavy scrutiny from longtime patrons for conducting Beethoven's famous 9th Symphony while facing the orchestra.

One patron, Lance Humphrey, told EOTT that he was offended that Chen did not conduct facing the audience like their old maestro. "Look, I understand that the symphony is still the symphony no matter what, but I just think that turning his back toward us while conducting takes us back to an archaic time."

Many have reportedly labeled Chen a "Rad Trad," saying that he was out of touch with mainstream music. Longtime parishioner Cecilia Cotes says that it reminds her of times when she would be in music class and would be "whacked on the knuckles with a violin bow."

"It's completely outdated," Cotes said. "What we want is Maestro Chen to turn and face us so that we can feel like we're participating in the orchestral movements. Does that make sense?"

At press time, Chen had said that he would not turn to face the people, but would consider allowing a number of patrons on stage to turn the pages of the sheet music during concerts.

Man Angry That Only Women Can Become Female Priests

Speaking at a Women's Rights group at the home of fellow parishioner Florence Hensley of Medford, Oregon this week, 58-year-old Roger Shannahan complained that the group was being sexist for unjustly excluding men from the group's hopes of a female priesthood.

"I mean, you could see in the early Church numbers of male figures who held positions of authority," Shannahan told the group. "St. Paul was a man, for instance. He had authority, right? So, if St. Paul was a man and had authority, why wouldn't I be able to have it?" Hensley, who hosts the weekly Women's Rights group, told EOTT after the meeting that men cannot be considered, not because men are unequal, only because it is not in a man's nature to become a female priest. But Shannahan believes otherwise, telling EOTT that the group has always overlooked men simply because of the group's own insecurities.

"I'm sick and tired of sitting on the sidelines. I, too, have a voice."

Study: 92% of Single Catholics Stop Praying for Spouse Mere Seconds before God Answers Prayer

In a new study published today by The League Of Single Catholics, nearly 93% of all Catholics quit praying for a spouse, or show signs of doubt in God's love, just seconds before He would have given them the man or woman of their lives.

According to Robin Longwood, who headed the study, more than nine out of ten single Catholics decide to stop praying either because they've been praying for someone to love for years and are ready to give up, or simply because they just need a break from the eight-hour "prayer-for-love" marathon they were in the midst of, just seconds, or minutes at most, before they would have bumped into their knight in shining armor or damsel at a grocery store or some other random place.

"Our research shows that most women who take a moment away from praying for a spouse to eat or sleep or to focus on work, would've just then, had she just not decided to eat, stumbled on a rock, and nearly plummet off a cliff before the man God had in mind for her would have taken out his rosary and lassoed it around her, caught her, and pulled her back into his manly, devout Catholic arms."

Longwood's advice to all single Catholics is to quit their jobs and to get as little sleep as possible so as to devote all their time to God, and to not miss their one true chance at love, because another study the League of Single Catholics conducted showed that "99% of Catholics only have one chance at happiness, and so must be vigilant so as not to screw it up."

Lazy Priest Institutes General Counseling

Explaining to his congregation that there was simply no time in the day to council the multitude of parishioners who needed spiritual guidance, Fr. Greg Barmes of Our Lady of the Parish announced that he was simply going to council everyone in the parish at once.

"I understand how difficult the situation must be for you!" Barmes yelled to all those gathered for counseling. "You must remember that the Lord loves you and can never forget you! What's that? Ah, yes, I understand that you feel like God's not there sometimes! But you must persevere through this dark night of the soul!"

Parishioner Jennifer Hall told EOTT that she usually had to wait up to two weeks to get an appointment with Barmes.

"Usually we have to wait two or three weeks to get an appointment so that we can listen to him give us advice about praying and trusting God and other things we're not gonna follow through with. It's really cool to listen to the advice from a priest with a hundred or so people as we collectively nod our heads and pretend we're gonna follow through with his suggestions."

"**U**sually we have to wait two or three weeks to get an appointment so that we can listen to him give us advice about praying and trusting God and other things we're not gonna follow through with. It's really cool to listen to the advice from a priest with a hundred or so people as we collectively nod our heads and pretend we're gonna follow through with his suggestions."

Permanent Deacon Has Assistant

Walking into St. John of the Cross Parish office to deliver their marriage certificate this week, newly wedded Jack and Helen Trumble confirmed that Deacon Donald Mathers has, for some reason, an assistant.

"We were actually shocked when we learned he had a desk of his own," said Jack Trumble. "But then we noticed he, God only knows why, actually had an office too...with his name on the door. We thought that was kinda weird seeing as how he's, you know, a deacon. No offense or anything... I mean, I know it's an important role and everything, but an office?"

"And that wasn't all," Helen Trumble continued in place of her baffled husband. "The man actually has an assistant. I mean, am I missing something here? He works fulltime as a checkout clerk at the grocery store down the street. And here he has an assistant? It's like he has this alternate universe thing going on."

At press time, the Matherses had overheard his assistant tell another visitor that the Deacon was booked for the day, but that the parish priest was free to speak with her.

Happy-Go-Lucky Priest Obviously Not Aware Most of Parishioners Going to Hell

According to daily communicants at the Church of St. Paul, the parish pastor happily greeting parishioners and playfully ruffling their children's hair must have absolutely no clue that most of his parishioners are going to suffer the fires of eternal damnation.

"Come here, you!" Fr. Rob Donovan jokingly said to a child as he hid behind his parents, clearly unaware or completely delusional to the fact that, judging by his jubilation and carefree attitude, he had to be in utter denial that he had given up marriage and kids to save souls, but hadn't once mentioned sin from the pulpit in the past two decades. "Oh, you're not gonna come say hi! OK, I see how it is."

"You, little buddy, are gonna get a water balloon right to the face next time I see you," he laughed as many parishioners within earshot could be easily heard talking in a manner that was at complete odds with what they had heard in the gospel reading.

"To hell with him, man...charge him twenty-percent interest," he must've misheard a parishioner who was standing directly behind him say, and thus, conveniently keeping intact his deranged mind from the reality that most of the people standing around him, in due time, were to be damned to the fires of hell, where they would spend eternity wailing and gnashing their teeth.

At press time, yeah, that one was kinda dark and judgmental, I know.

Frustrated New Priest Still Hasn't Nailed down Consecration

Sadly admitting he had yet to figure out how other priests "did it," newly ordained priest Fr. Christian Benson told EOTT this morning that he was still struggling with "the whole consecration part."

"I got the entrance and opening down, and I do a pretty decent job with the homily and all the rest, but the consecration, I don't know... I just can't grasp how to transubstantiate," said Benson, who, at his most recent attempt at the consecration lifted the chalice as he said, "this is my body."

"Last week I gave such a stirring homily about the reality of abortion that afterwards, there wasn't a dry eye in the church. But then I got to the consecration, tried a few times, then just called it quits."

Speaking to Bensen's seminary instructor early this afternoon, Fr. Thomas Dewall told EOTT that, although Benson's oratory skills reminded him of a slightly more captivating St. John Chrysostom, his piety rivaled that of St. John the Evangelist, and his knowledge made Thomas Aquinas sound like a mere buffoon, Bensen, for some reason, had trouble with following the instructions when it came to the consecration.

"I honestly don't know what to say," Dewall said. "Just the other day I looked at his hands and realized he had the stigmata. But for some reason he still can't get down the Words of Institution. It's like he freezes when he gets to that part."

"I honestly don't know what to say," Dewall said. "Just the other day I looked at his hands and realized he had the stigmata. But for some reason he still can't get down the Words of Institution. It's like he freezes when he gets to that part."

Nuns on Bus Scour Ohio in Search of Misplaced Veils

A group of Catholic nuns began a 1,000-mile bus tour through Ohio this week asking locals whether or not they have seen their veils.

The group of about twenty nuns departed Cincinnati early Wednesday morning after every single one of them realized that they had not seen their veils in over four decades. The youngest of the group, Sister Mary Fleischer, 79, told EOTT that losing things had become all too familiar for the group lately, joking, "I just hope we don't lose our minds next." Then, turning to a complete stranger, said, "Isn't that just the darndest thing? Honestly, I could of sworn I left it right here. Wait a minute, you're not my son. I don't even have a son. Who am I?"

Feminist Nun Wondering Whether It Best to Leave Wife to Become Priestess

Explaining to EOTT this morning that she knew the moment would sooner or later arrive when she would be forced to make the tough decision between remaining with her longtime partner, or leaving her to completely focus on becoming a member of the clergy, local feminist and nun Sister Margaret Ramsay acknowledged the fact that the decision was tougher than expected.

"I know the life that God has chosen for me is a tough one, but this is much more difficult than the time I decided to take the veil, Ramsay told EOTT in an exclusive interview. "It's definitely much easier than the time I decided to remove the veil. Not many things in my life have been easier than that."

Ramsay went on to say that even compared to the time she decided to marry longtime friend Janice Worland, which went against her vows as a nun and Catholic, this one "was a toughy."

"I mean, yes, technically the Church still hasn't yet allowed female ordination, but that's nothing to me. God has allowed it. More, He has called me to it. Just as He called me to take the veil, and just as He called me to remove it so as to be one with society. And now He has called me to wear the cleric, which I gladly accept. But the question remains; do I leave my lady partner? It seems the most responsible thing to do. I mean, how weird would a priestess look walking around with a girlfriend?"

At press time, Ramsay had decided to leave her girlfriend so as not to scandalize the faithful.

POPES & PEOPLE

"The thing about alcohol is that it affects your ability to recognize how many times Scott Hahn uses the word 'covenant.'"

New Scott Hahn Drinking Game Has Readers Taking Shot after Every Mention of Word "Covenant"

A new, dangerous drinking game known as *Covenant*, invented by Franciscan University of Steubenville sophomore Ben Johnson, is sweeping Catholic universities. The game, which involves players reading any book ever published by Scott Hahn, and then taking a shot of whiskey or beer every time the word "covenant" is mentioned, is raising major concerns with university officials.

What originally started out as fun for some has now turned dangerous, officials are reporting, with one man listed in critical condition and at least forty-seven others being admitted to area hospitals for alcohol poisoning. Now health professionals are warning Catholics of the dangers of playing *Covenant*.

"This is one of, if not *the* most, lethal games I've ever come across," said Dr. Candice Jarvis, medical adviser to the USCCB. "The thing about alcohol is that it affects your ability to recognize how many times Scott Hahn uses the word 'covenant,' and it absolutely affects your ability to ask the question of whether or not there are any synonyms of the word he could be using. You go into the game thinking the word will be read two or three times, and next thing you know you're on your twenty-sixth shot after just a few paragraphs. I'd even venture to say that it would be safer if students took a shot after every mention of the word 'the.'"

Game creator Ben Johnson told EOTT this morning that the

game is admittedly more dangerous and "way crazier" than the Rick Warren drinking game he played when he was an Evangelical. "In that game we'd chug Pepsi every time we came across the word 'Purpose.' The worst thing I ever witnessed playing that game was people getting major sugar highs."

At press time, Scott Hahn had urged students to consider the potential "prophets and losses" of playing *Covenant*.

Matt Fradd Named Eye of the Tiber's Sexiest Chastity Speaker Alive

Eye of the Tiber is happy to announce that Catholic apologist Matt Fradd has been named its Sexiest Chastity Speaker Alive. His rugged good looks, dirty blond locks, and of course the masculine, yet somehow soft and gentle sound of this Aussie's voice helped make him this year's top choice. Although this Australian by birth, Catholic by choice hottie spends his time preparing for talks on subjects such as chastity, love, and the dangers of pornography, there's no need for this Australian Stallion to ever prepare to look handsome. "When it comes to his face, it seems as though time has stopped at five o'clock in the afternoon," EOTT Fashion Correspondent Janice Debuke recently told the press. "Combine his perpetual five o'clock shadow with his somewhat disheveled, dirty, dirty-blond hair, while staring into his refined and stately eyes, and you'll find yourself hypnotized by the end of his talk."

After being notified of this win, Fradd thanked EOTT on their decision, and went on to thank those nominated with him. "I just felt so honored to even be named in the same category as Chris Stefanik," Fradd told EOTT in the typical modest fashion that helped him win the award.

At press time EOTT had received a one-word message from Stefanik: "Bull."

Pope Francis Washes Feet of Eight Men, One Woman, a Muslim, Ferret, and a Double Amputee

Pope Francis visited the Don Gnocchi Center in Rome today to wash the feet of twelve residents for the Holy Week ritual.

According to the Catholic Information Service, those twelve included one woman, a Muslim, a pet ferret named Wilbur, and a double amputee, which falls in line with Pope Francis' actions during last year's Maundy Thursday.

The ceremony, which is rooted in the story of the Last Supper, made headlines last year when the pope visited a youth detention center and washed the feet of anyone who happened to be in his proximity.

Deputy CEO and Director of Policy and Programs at Good Works Incorporated, Alessandria Stefanoni, told Vatican Radio the Pope has shown a commitment to bringing attention to those most often forgotten in society, including the disabled, four-legged mammals, and nearly anything else that was created by God. "It is giving a voice," Stefanoni said. "It's showing respect for their dignity."

In November, Pope Francis critiqued society's tendency to "hide physical fragility," which he rejected by greeting hundreds of people in wheelchairs and encouraging them to become "protagonists" in the Catholic church. He also critiqued society's tendency to discriminate against mammals belonging to the weasel genus of the family Mustelidae.

Catholic League's William Donohue
Offended about Something

It is being reported to EOTT at this hour that Catholic League President, William Donohue, may possibly be offended about something.

Daylight Savings News: Sedevacantist Family Moves Clocks Back Seven Centuries

After having recently set the family clock back seven centuries for daylight savings time, patriarch of a local sedevacantist family told EOTT this morning that, although he was excited about having moved the clock back to "a better time," it was still weird getting used to the time change.

"Oh, it's always weird trying to adjust to a time change," said a sick Jeremy Miller as he tried to fight off a bout with the Black Plague. "Especially when you're adjusting your clock to a time when the Mass was said properly and people had morals and were happy. Still, it's a change when you're used to the sun being out for longer. Your body and mind really need to get used to the facts that it's going to get dark earlier, and that if you have to defecate, it's gonna have to be in a disease-infested bucket. I guess the good thing is that you gain a few centuries of sleep, which you really need if you're gonna find the energy and strength to survive the Great Famine which is killing millions of people as we speak."

Miller went on to report that, although he was beginning to enjoy the time change, it was still odd to hear himself being referred to as "old man" at the age of 36.

NASA Discovers Earth-Like Planet That Could Support Maryknoll Fathers

NASA astronomers today revealed that they have discovered an Earth-like planet close to 600 light-years away that might be able to sustain the Maryknoll Fathers and Brothers.

Roughly Earth-sized, the planet called Kepler-196g orbits a star from a distance scientists call the "habitable zone," the range at which it could have liquid water for Maryknoll Fathers to survive, without them having to be on the same planet as other Catholics to do so.

"We have found that this is the optimal distance any Catholic should be from some Maryknoll Fathers and Brothers," Jason Cleft, research scientist with the Kepler Science Team at NASA, told EOTT. "If we could find a way to get them there, we would be looking at just the right buffer. If any of them tried to mention something about women priests, it would take 600 light-years for that message of dissent to reach Earth. We also believe that if they attempted to mail us a shipment of *Maryknoll Magazines*, that the shipment would burn up in the atmosphere before it ever reached us."

The Kepler Space Telescope has already discovered close to two-dozen other planets that could possibly support the Maryknoll Fathers, but those are all only 400 light-years away, making them what one church official called, "Still too close for comfort."

Breaking: Priests Smiling, Laughing during Mass Remains Leading Obstacle to SSPX Reunion

According to a new study released by the Vatican today, the leading obstacle to full reconciliation with the Society of St. Pius X remains whether or not priests ought to be allowed to smile and/or laugh while saying Mass.

The commission set up to investigate the possibility of reunion with the traditionalist organization said in their report that priests moving about the altar like robots that could possibly, with the slightest amount of water, short circuit mid-Mass is a hallmark of Society priests.

"A large sticking point is Vatican II, obviously," said lead commission researcher Thomas Daniels. "Their ability to walk, mechanically, about the sanctuary as though in search of a can of oil to lubricate their gears is paramount, and we understand that. They don't want anyone, including the Vatican, to tell them what joint or gears in their robotic bodies to oil up. They have already stated that due to the fact that anything that takes away people's focus on every intricate motion and movement in the Mass is of utmost importance, smiling is naturally a sin, and therefore cannot be forced upon them."

Pope Emeritus Benedict XVI Asks
to Be Reinstated as Pope

According to reports today, Pope Emeritus Benedict XVI is seeking the chair of his pontificate months after his resignation. The news has sent shock waves around the world.

Vatican spokesman Fr. Vitateli Devitiamani told EOTT that, "[Benedict] came for a dinner as scheduled and then proceeded to return to his old living quarters. That wouldn't be a problem, since His Holiness Pope Francis chose to live elsewhere, the room is open. However, once we asked him where he was going, he simply said, 'I'm back,' then proceeded to put his sunglasses on even though we were inside."

Sources say that the next morning, he walked down the hall asking for his valet and his red shoes, and was overheard asking an adviser to "get Burke on the line."

EOTT had the chance to sit down with the Pope Emeritus to discuss the ordeal.

"You have to understand that, months ago, I received a call from Word of Fire Catholic Ministries. It was Fr. Steve Grunow on the phone along with his colleague Jared Zimmerer. They're both serious about the care of the body and the mind, and offered to help me regain some strength in both. I gratefully accepted. So, after months of training, I've lost weight, regained my muscle mass and strength of mind. I've never felt better. And to tell you the truth, I never actually filed the paperwork to officially exit my office," Benedict said just outside the Bernini

Columns where he proceeded to flick a lit cigarette into a full barrel of gasoline and walk away as the barrel exploded.

At press time, Benedict still hadn't looked back at the massive explosion.

Pope Francis to Work Midnight Shift at McDonald's to Help the Poor

The new Holy Father, after paying his hotel bill the day of his election to "give an example to priests," has decided to submit an application to work the midnight shift at the McDonald's on Via Del Corso in order to "make a few extra clams" to give to the poor.

"My children, as St. Paul reminded the Thessalonians: 'For you remember our labor and toil, brethren; we worked night and day, that we might not burden any of you, while we preached to you the gospel of God.' I also, taking his example, wish to toil, in order to raise funds for a new couch that this one guy really needs."

The manager at the McDonald's who reviewed the Holy Father's application, stated that the Pope was, "ridiculously over-qualified" for the job, but added, "but like, he's the Pope. How exactly do you say no to him?"

At press time, His Holiness had reportedly sold three Big Macs to Cardinal Sandri of the Congregation for the Eastern Churches, and then proceeded to kneel and ask for his blessing.

"Life on the Rock" Inexplicably Picked up for yet Another Season

The EWTN program *Life On The Rock* was inexplicably picked up for yet another season this week, baffling many of its viewers as well as network CEO, Michael Warsaw. A source at the network announced this week that "for absolutely no good reason whatsoever" they have decided to pick up the show for teens and young adults for another season.

"To be honest, I haven't the faintest clue why we keep doing this to our viewers," Warsaw said, laughing. "It started out years ago as an April Fools joke, and for some reason or other it just stuck." Warsaw went on to say that, though the program is painful in itself, it *has* had some good effects on its "Catholic Militant viewership." "From the outset of each program the viewer is made to watch and listen to the theme song, which can be used as a means to purge the soul of sins, so we believe."

But one viewer, a former agnostic who asked to remain anonymous, told EOTT that the program has done nothing but question his belief in all that is good and beautiful. "I just...I don't know. Sometimes I just wonder how a good and loving God could allow something like this to happen...season after season."

Catholic Answers Runs out of Questions; To Close Its Doors in May

It was officially announced today that after twenty-five years, the largest lay-run Catholic apostolate for evangelization and apologetics in the United States, Catholic Answers, is closing its doors for good next May.

The decision to shut down the apostolate was revealed on a live broadcast of *The World Over* with Raymond Arroyo last week when, during the break, Catholic Answers founder, Karl Keating, was caught on a hot mic saying, "Honestly, though, I'm kinda over it. I mean, how many times during Lent do I have to be asked whether frog legs are considered meat?"

63-year-old Keating spoke to the press after the interview and apologized to anyone he may have offended. "Here's the thing...we've pretty much answered everything there is to answer. Simply put, we've run out of questions."

The apostolate is expected to close its doors after releasing its final issue of *Catholic Answers Magazine*, in which the topic of the proper amount of incense required during a Chaldean Rite liturgy is discussed. "Yup...that'll pretty much wrap it up," Keating said.

Pope's Peace Doves Attacked by Metaphors

In a gesture at the Vatican's annual "Caravan of Peace," Pope Francis happily watched as two children at his side released a pair of white doves as symbols of peace and unity from the window of the Apostolic Palace.

But just moments later, two crows, metaphors of the world's unwillingness for dialogue and its utter hostility at the thought of compromise, swept down on the hapless symbols of peace as tens of thousands of people in St. Peter's Square looked on.

One dove managed to break free from one of the metaphors, losing a few feathers in the brawl, symbolizing that, though the chance of peace in the world is not dead, it is severely fragile to more dominant and negative attitudes. A crow playing the metaphor of the world's hostility toward compromise had a better grip on the other dove, pecking the symbol of peace repeatedly, reminding all those gathered that in the face of hatred, there really is not much of a chance for peace anywhere in the world, let alone the Middle East.

In the end, both symbols of peace got away, although the extent of their injuries was not immediately clear.

The boy looked upset at the bird's misfortune, prompting the pope to embrace him and pat his head. The young girl appeared to be cynically laughing at the sudden turn of events, perhaps realizing for the first time in her short life that achieving peace is doomed to violence and struggle against the oppression of tyrants and Muslim terrorists.

USCCB to Consider Implementing Challenge Flags and Instant Replays during Masses

As bishops from across the country gather in Washington, D.C. this weekend for the annual USCCB Liturgical Conference, many within the Church are speculating about rumors that U.S. bishops may vote on a proposal to implement instant replay for every Mass starting next year.

The idea of using instant replay cameras during Mass was first proposed in 2009 by then Archbishop of New York, Timothy Dolan. "I believe that technology could actually be an immense benefit to us," Dolan told EOTT in a 2009 interview. "The idea would be to give a red challenge flag to two or three parishioners to toss onto the sanctuary on behalf of the congregation should they feel something heretical, or something not in line with the rubrics of the Mass had occurred. They would not have ability to throw the flag in the case of an overtly fluffy homily. Once the Liturgy of the Eucharist had begun, all reviews could only then come from upstairs, so to speak."

But some critics of instant replays, such as 47-year-old Mary Collins from New Haven, Connecticut, say that implementing such a move would mean prolonged Masses. "Mass already takes so long," Collins told reporters. "Also, there's just something special about the human element in Mass... You never know what could happen. It's kinda exciting."

Rival Knights of Columbus Councils Clash Swords over Territory

Rival councils of the Knights of Columbus clashed with one another on Friday at Our Lady of Good Intentions parish hall in Orlando, Florida, officials have confirmed. At least twelve Knights were injured.

"We believe that the clash may have started after two Knights of Columbus field agents attempted to sell life insurance to the same prospective client," said Supreme Council Insurance Director, Gerry Kaur.

Television images showed dramatic footage of two groups of Knights clad in white feathered caps and red capes rushing into the church with wheelchairs and walkers to assist their fellow field agents, brandishing their swords against each other.

"It was like the slowest battle ever," one eyewitness told EOTT. "Imagine watching *Braveheart* in slowmo. It was actually kinda cute."

"The fact is that each field agent has his own territory," said Vice Supreme Master Donny Bagwin as he devoured a still-beating heart. "We're currently investigating whose territory it belonged to. If it's proven that one of the field agents *was* selling life insurance in a territory that was not his own, he will be flogged or racked. Of course, you will not be able to witness it if you're not a Knight, so I encourage you to take a look into becoming one. We have many great benefits." Bagwin went on to speak about the history of the Knights for two and a half hours as he wiped blood off his sword.

Another eyewitness reported hearing one of the councils shouting slogans against the other council as they charged. "I don't remember word for word what was said, but I think it had something to do with annuities. And another knight was screaming to another that it was finally time to 'make use of his life insurance policy' as he wildly swung his sword."

No arrests have been made at this time.

Francis "Much Better Pope Than That Other Guy We Had," Area Nominal Catholic Reports

Telling his son that,"This new pope guy is much better than that other one," earlier this afternoon, area Catholic Bernard Ripley stressed to his son the immense difference he saw in regards to the papacy of "this Francis guy," as opposed to "the other guy who was pope before retiring."

"That other pope, what's-his-face, was too stuck in the past," said Ripley, who reportedly has not attended Mass since his son was born twenty years ago. "He hardly ever talked, and when he did, he was always wanting to take us back to the middle evil ages or something." Ripley went on to report to his son that if the Church did not want to become a thing of the past, they would have to get with the times. "I guess that's the thing. This guy Francis has really got it down. The Church is real scared of his teachings. You know he's gonna ordain women and let men priests have sex? Yeah, he's changing things, this guy."

Critics Call Scott Hahn's Latest Book
"Lots of Pun to Read"

Ignatius Press has announced that Scott Hahn's upcoming book will be loaded from start to finish with laugh-out-loud, side-splitting, yet thought-provoking puns. "With this book, I've managed to fully explore the way humor and moral theology compliment one another," explained Hahn in an exclusive interview with EOTT. "The results are simply pun-tastic."

Hahn, known for his heavy use of puns, said that his new book on Capital Punishment, titled, *Capital Pun-ishment: A Light Look at a Grave Matter,* has taken theology and wit to a whole new level. "Does it really do us any good to get 'hung up' on propriety when discussing capital punishment?" asks Hahn. "If you find something 'shocking' about an electric chair joke, then maybe you could use an 'injection' of humor. And that's what this book will provide. These are all original puns that I came up with myself," Dr. Hahn added with a smile. "So, I guess you could say this was a 'Hahn-solo' project."

University of Steubenville Quarterback Exclusively Throwing "Hail Marys"

Franciscan University of Steubenville, best known for their strict adherence to the Magisterium of the Catholic Church, has decided that their football playbook will continue to contain no other play but the "Hail Mary."

"Even in football we're called to heed the words of St. Paul when he says, 'Pray without ceasing,'" University President Reverend Terence Henry told EOTT just moments after he released every running back and tight end from the roster. "No matter the situation, our quarterback will continue to exclusively throw a 'Hail Mary.' And in this way shall we proclaim the power of the Rosary."

While some have criticized Henry, calling his eccentric decision to continue to limit his playbook to "Hail Marys" nothing more than a publicity stunt for the small Catholic college, Henry believes otherwise. "Look...people only tend to pray in desperate situations, and that's wrong... So why only use this play in desperate situations? All we're trying to do is to show people that just as you ought to pray without ceasing, so then should you also use this play without ceasing...you following me?"

The radical decision made for a humiliating defeat in a game last month against Ave Maria University when, with Steubenville down by three points with one second left in the game and just one yard from the end zone, quarterback Rich Vaughan stepped

back to pass and launched the football through the uprights and
clear into the stands.

Pope Attends Charismatic Prayer Service to Experience What Torture Feels Like

Pope Francis led a pep rally yesterday in Rome's Olympic Stadium in front of more than 50,000 Catholics who follow charismatic movements.

While listening to what many have termed "the most heinous music ever prayed to," 50,000 Catholics raised their hands in unison as they prayed for Francis, who silently and repeatedly asked God Almighty to "just make it stop."

Francis told the faithful that the devil wants to destroy the family, which he described as the "domestic church," and went on to plead for the end of the use of torture.

"We also call on the international community to put a stop to the torture of prisoners. I'm guessing that this is why this music is playing in the background. That we may know what it is to suffer excruciating pain."

Francis told the crowd that when he was the Buenos Aires archbishop, at first he didn't "share" the way the exuberant charismatic Catholics prayed there, but now realized that he still has not changed his mind, going on to encourage everyone to man up and stop crying already.

Many in the crowd, we think, told EOTT while speaking in tongues that they were thrilled by the visit, saying, "Я тоже не знаю, что говорю." Another woman said that "In realta', non so quello che sto facendo adesso," while her husband concurred with whatever the heck his wife had just said, adding, "Ich glaube, ich bete für euch gerade jetzt, aber ich kann nicht sicher sein."

"It was wonderful to see him there," said Donetta Corti, a charismatic Catholic living in Rome, as she swayed back and forth with one hand in the air like some doped up hippie just moments after taking a hit of that sweet, sweet ganja. "The entire experience appeared to overwhelm His Holiness as it does most every newcomer. Many times you could see him slumped over, vomiting, and asking God to just stop it and to put him out of his misery. It was obvious the man wanted to die a martyr. What humility…to plead to God because the pain and suffering in the world touches him at such a deep level."

Toward the end of the event, Francis invited members of the charismatic movement to the Vatican for a prayer service, adding that there were many people in the curia and Vatican Bank whom he would like to have "sit through this" as a warning to never act out of line again.

EWTN Announces New Reality Show Lineup

Addressing the latest ratings dip for EWTN, the network's president and CEO, Michael Warsaw, announced today that the station would be making some radical changes to its upcoming lineup.

Following the lead of other popular television networks like MTV and VH1, EWTN unveiled its all new reality show lineup set to premier this fall. Shows already turning heads include, *So You Think You Can Pray*, *America's Next Top Extraordinary Minister*, and *Lead Us Not Into Temptation Island*.

EWTN unveiled its all new reality show lineup set to premier this fall. Shows already turning heads include, *So You Think You Can Pray*, *America's Next Top Extraordinary Minister*, and *Lead Us Not Into Temptation Island*.

Pope Francis Awaiting Final Approval of Internet Troll before Promulgating Encyclical

Vatican sources are confirming that Pope Francis has nearly completed his new encyclical letter, and is awaiting the final approval of Reginald Edwards, an internet troll commonly known as "PiusXIIRoxII."

Edwards, who has read several paragraphs of the Catechism, three books by Peter Kreeft, and half of St. John Paul II's "Fides et Ratio," is universally regarded as the final authority in matters of Orthodoxy in internet chatrooms, forums, and the comment section under YouTube videos.

Speaking from the kitchen this morning, Reginald's mother told EOTT over a phone interview: "I'm so proud of Reggie for getting to be a consultant to the Vatican. He's more than earned it. All he does is sit in the basement on his computer, answering questions and demanding people justify their beliefs to him. He gets so into it that he often locks the door and doesn't let me down there, even to bring him lemonade."

Edwards has already made several notes on the new encyclical, titled *Bora et Labora*, having circled or underlined several paragraphs in red and written margin notes such as "a little too Spirit of Vatican-II-ey" and "where is this in the Catechism?"

Pope Michael Comes to Aid of Deposed Nigerian Prince; Transfers "Sum of USD 5 Millions"

Speaking from his porcelain throne yesterday, Pope Michael announced to those gathered in the papal living room that, as a sign of unity between the church and the great people of Nigeria, he would be transferring the "sum of USD 5 millions" to an anonymous deposed Nigerian prince.

Citing an email he received just days prior, Pope Michael told those gathered that his heart went out to the Nigerian prince, and to *all* the royalty suffering in the world. "I've received many of these emails in the past few months. This seems like an all too common issue, and it's time that it's addressed." Michael went on to criticize "the so-called Pope in Rome" for his inaction and hypocrisy in such issues. "He tells the world to live modestly, but a Christian is called to live modestly by his own free will, not by being forced, as is in this case where the heavy hand of government officials who set up companies and awarded themselves contracts which are grossly over-invoiced in various ministries, or something like that," he said, trying to make sense of the email.

At press time, Michael had directed his mother as Secretary of State to please acknowledge the receipt of the email and to await detailed information of the pending project as instructed.

Tensions Escalate as North Korea Threatens to Deploy LCWR Nuns on West

Defense Secretary Chuck Hagel is calling North Korea's threat to use LCWR nuns strapped to long-range missiles a "provocative action" and a "growing threat" to the U.S. and its allies.

In a telephone call to EOTT Tuesday evening, Hagel cited North Korea's pursuit of nuclear weapons and ballistic missiles as "nothing compared to the threat of one more nun from the Leadership Conference of Women Religious successfully reaching the mainland."

"We need to do everything in our power to stop the North Korean threat before we get to the point of no return," Hagel said. "What we fear is a miscalculation that leads to a provocation."

North Korea has recently stated that they have the ability to attach an LCWR nun to a long-range missile that could target South Korea and the U.S. mainland. "From there, who knows what damage the nun would inflict. Thousands...tens of thousands of innocent television viewers could be in danger of having to watch as the nun is inevitably interviewed by CNN. We have enough of them here as it is, and the officials in Pyongyang know this. One more of them could break the Church in the U.S. When the Church goes, so does the last vestiges of culture, and finally, the U.S. would crumble as well. It's a slow, painful death."

Russian Orthodox Church Forced to Acknowledge Papal Supremacy after Losing Game of Poker to Pope

Russian Orthodox Primate Kirill of Moscow has officially acknowledged the Pope as head of the Christian Church after losing on a straight to a flush, sources are confirming.

Authorities in Moscow confirmed reports today that in the early hours of Saturday morning, Russian Orthodox Primate Kirill lost a poker bet to Pope Francis after forgetting that a straight beats a flush, leading to Kirill losing the Russian Orthodox Church to the Vatican.

"I always freaking forget that," Kirill told EOTT as he knelt to kiss the Pope's ring. "I always forget that flush beats straight, I don't know why. I couldn't exactly ask about the rules at that point of the game, could I? He'd know right away what I had. Anyhow, I didn't bet, just checked so that I could find some freaking time to figure out whether I had him or not, but he...excuse me...His Holiness bet 65,000,000 rubles and his papal ring."

Kirill went on to say that, though he was beginning to remember that a flush would beat his straight, he wasn't completely sure, and had to bet due to the fact that he was "pot committed."

"I would like to apologize to all the Russian faithful," Kirill said in a statement at the Vatican this morning. "Good news is that I have found that the Roman Church does, in fact, contain the fullness of truth. Bad news is that some of you Russian priests must learn American folk songs for the Liturgy. Either that, or wear a clown nose while saying the Consecration. I'm not sure...still trying to figure this whole western thing out."

The Dark Lord Sauron to Head Upcoming LCWR Annual Assembly

Sister Florence Deacon announced today that the upcoming annual assembly for the Leadership Conference of Women Religious would be taking place at the smoldering base of Mount Doom in Mordor, and would be led by the Dark Lord Sauron.

The announcement came in a joint statement between LCWR leaders and numerous well known officials from the lands surrounding Mordor including Azog the Defiler, Uruk-hai Scout Captain Ugluk, Orc Captain of the Warg Rider Sharku, and President of LCWR Carol Zinn. LCWR and Mordor leaders would not comment on the specifics of the upcoming conference except to say that they were eagerly anticipating the conference, which would focus on LCWR's ongoing situation with the Vatican.

"We shall soon celebrate the dawn of a new era!" Zinn shouted to tens of thousands of cheering Orcs and LCWR nuns as they all furiously, mindlessly slammed their spears against their shields in unison, over and over again. Zinn went on to conclude her rousing speech, shouting, "One conference to rule us all! No habits to bind us! No veil to blind us! And with liberation at our helm shall they be defied!"

Lila Rose Goes Undercover as Fetus

In an astounding show of acting determination and dexterity, President of the anti-abortion organization *Live Action,* Lila Rose, went undercover as a fetus at an area Planned Parenthood this week.

Rose, best known for going undercover as a 15-year-old pregnant girl desperately seeking options at local Planned Parenthoods, premiered her latest video on *The O'Reilly Factor* last night.

"I couldn't believe it...I'm still in shock," a Planned Parenthood nurse said. "I mean, first I'm looking at the sonogram and next thing you know there's a fetus waving at me and holding a sign saying, 'I'm a human life.'"

Two witnesses at the scene were taken to the hospital after fainting. They are being treated for minor cuts and bruises.

In an astounding show of acting determination and dexterity, President of the anti-abortion organization *Live Action,* Lila Rose, went undercover as a fetus at an area Planned Parenthood this week.

Knights of Columbus Totally Not Catholic Version of Freemasons

The Knights of Columbus, which are made up of wealthy white men and organized into Jurisdictions, Districts, and Councils boasting of over 14,000 local units in America alone, were founded by Fr. Michael J. McGivney, who was totally a real person and whose real name was, no joke, "McGivney," with the mission, "to prevent Catholic men from entering secret societies whose membership was antithetical to Church teaching."

Upon entrance, a new Knight is given the title "First Degree" during a ceremony to which no one who is not a member is invited. After serving in the Knights for a certain unspecified amount of time and attending their meetings (which are not closed off except to those who have not gained membership in the Knights), the member enters the "Second Degree" by partaking in a ritual service which is entirely open to all who are members of the Knights of Columbus. Similar events happen during the "Third" and "Fourth" degree ceremonies.

"Joining the Knights of Columbus is quite simple," said Second Degree Knight Robert Burkens. "One simply must be a male, over eighteen, and Catholic, and current Knights will seek him out and badger him to join, treating him as somehow not truly Catholic until he does. The insurance policy is completely optional, but recommended, since soon-to-be St. John Paul II was once quoted as saying, 'The Knights of Columbus Insurance Policy is the right hand of the Catholic Church.'"

St. Clare Press Ready to Publish New
Non-Confrontational Translation of Bible

Catholic book publisher and distributor St. Clare Press announced today that their new non-confrontational translation of the Bible will be released sometime this September.

St. Clare executive Roger Hammond told the press this week that he hopes the new translation will help to appease the minds of critics who have long called the Bible violent and judgmental.

"It took close to a decade to complete this ambitious translation, and we're confident it'll help people better understand the all-encompassing compassion contained within the scriptures. Hammond goes on to explain one of the most riveting scenes in the New Testament where Jesus, after having overturned the tables of the money changers, goes back to help clean up, apologizing profusely as he does so. Another scene in which the compassion and kindness of Jesus shines forth is Matthew 16:23 where, after having been asked by Peter to not enter Jerusalem and eventually fall into the hands of the Pharisees, Jesus asks Peter to *"hold that thought for a moment,"* before addressing Satan: *"Satan, if you wouldn't mind could you move just a tad bit behind me? I'd really like to get this little point across to Peter. I feel so rude asking you this, but... I mean, don't go out of your way or anything..."*

Hammond went on to tell reporters that the project has become a kind of therapy for all those involved in the project. One employee of St. Clare Press, Beverly Tomas, said that seeing

Christ in a new, more tender, and compassionate way helped her get over years of abuse she suffered by "strict and judgmental nuns." "I remember sitting back just a year ago and reading a newly translated verse in which the old Christ would've said something like 'Woe to you, Pharisees, you hypocrites,' but now he gently places a hand on the shoulder of a Pharisee, pleadingly, and says, *'Come on, guy... I was gonna call you whited-washed sepulchers, but honestly, I don't think you're all that bad... I just think maybe you're hurting,' and lightly tapping the Pharisee on the chest, Jesus said unto him, 'Hey, guy... you wanna know what I think? I think you're hurting inside... hurting right there in that big ol' heart of yours. Is that why you're acting like this? Wanna talk about it?'"*

Head of Opus Dei Reaffirms Prelature Not a Cult

Bishop Javier Echevarria Rodriguez, head of the Prelature of the Holy Cross and Opus Dei, countered what he called "unfair and ridiculous attacks" against Opus Dei on a local radio program this morning.

"Because of documentaries, the mainstream media, as well as books like *The Da Vinci Code*," he said, "far too many people have been seduced by the idea that we're Catholic Freemasons; a secret society manipulating the Church from within. But these are all lies."

The Spanish Bishop offered what he called "a better alternative" for finding out the truth of Opus Dei, asking those interested in finding out more about the prelature to remember that "Midnight is the mark...downtown, between 4th and B, where Palm does root beside stone crypts, and below which, inscribed epitaph does mark the point, a hooded man shall greet thee; follow him to the way the furrow and the forge."

"Sedevacantist Singles" Employees Not Sure Whether to Recognize Authority of Company President

After being called in to a meeting by *Sedevacantist Singles* President, Michael Hoffman, early Thursday morning, employees of the ultra-traditionalist dating site were perplexed as to whether to acknowledge their CEO's authority, and to attend the mandatory meeting, sources confirm.

"I'm just not sure whether to believe he's the real president," said Barbara Dolby, a new employee of the company. "Many of my coworkers say that our board of directors sold out when they implemented some weird policy changes that are at complete odds with what we stand for, such as allowing members to write their profiles in the vernacular. Therefore, the board never truly had the authority to choose our current president, Mr. Hoffman. Also, though I've only been here a couple weeks, I've noticed that [Michael Hoffman] *does* do a lot of modern crap during meetings, like making us all sit at an oval-shaped table in the boardroom so that we can see each other and 'better communicate.'"

At press time, Hoffman had received an email from one staffer saying in part that no employee would attend the meeting about boosting membership from its current number of three men and two women, until Hoffman consented to having all meetings done with his back toward the employees.

SSPX Acolyte Stumbles during Offertory; Mass Deemed Invalid

12-year-old acolyte Jake Brody atoned for his sin Sunday for having negligently, sinfully stumbled on his way to the altar earlier that morning.

The Mass was immediately stopped when the presiding priest, Robert Dillard, deemed it no longer valid. "It was just a mistake...I understand," Dillard admitted, but explained that stumbling did not appear anywhere in the 1962 missal. "Jake is making amends for his *culpa* as we speak, but he'll be replaced nevertheless for the next Mass."

When asked why such a seemingly trivial matter should result in a stoppage of Mass, Dillard responded, "What'd you just say?"

SSPX Excommunicates Renegade Bishop for Installing Bishops without Approval

SSPX Arizona Bishop Gerald Leif confirmed Thursday that he has installed four bishops in spite of SSPX forbiddance.

The move comes months after meetings collapsed between Bishop Leif and SSPX's Superior General, Bernard Fellay. Leif, a prominent critic of the Society's growing liberal view toward ecumenism, has denounced the Society's dialogue with the Vatican.

A spokesman for the Diocese of Arizona declined to comment, but did say that the four newly-appointed bishops would continue to acknowledge the authority of Bernard Fellay as supreme head of SSPX, but would defy the excommunication.

National Catholic Reporter Beats out
Eye of the Tiber for Best Catholic News Parody

Winners of the 10th annual National Catholic Awards were an-nounced last night at the Kodak Theatre in Hollywood. The star-studded event, which included Dr. Scott Hahn, Fr. Mitch Pakwa, and Cardinal Timothy Dolan, all eagerly awaited the night's most anticipated award for *Best Catholic News Parody*. As expected, the top prize went back to nine-time winner of the award, the National Catholic Reporter, who beat out Eye of the Tiber. The night's other big winners included Pope Michael who won for *Best Conclavist*, and Hans Kung for his portray-al of a Catholic scholar in *Autobiography of Hans Kung*.

Jesuit Celebrates Halloween by Dressing up In "Priest Costume"

Hoping to surprise his family and friends at Holy Trinity Parish's annual Halloween Breakfast this morning, local Jesuit Walter Allen arrived dressed as a Roman Catholic Priest.

"It's always been a fun little idea of mine to wear one of these things," Allen said, shortly after he surprised those gathered at the breakfast.

"He walked right up to us and asked if we wanted him to bless our food," Allen's mother, Suzy Allen, recalled, "but none of us had any clue that it was Walt in that thing, so we were like, 'sure, why not?'" But the Allen family soon became suspicious when Allen forgot the meal-time prayer midway through. "That's when we knew it was Walt," his mother said.

Thomas Aquinas College Offering New Two-Year Program in The "Pretty Good Books"

Thomas Aquinas College in Santa Paula, California announced this week that they will be offering a new two-year program in the *Pretty Good Books*.

The small liberal arts and sciences college, which is known for its fidelity to the Magisterium of the Catholic Church as well as its focus on Great Books, is now offering a new program designed for students whose minds are not yet quite prepared for the good books, let alone the great ones.

President of the college, Michael McLean, told EOTT that the purpose of the ambitious new program is that it can be used as "a stepping stone to the better works in history."

"I believe that our students are not only some of the most faithful students in the country, but they're also some of the brightest minds in the Church. But we're looking to be a little more inclusive now. We're looking for orthodox students who do not have bright minds, but nevertheless have the potential of becoming bright minds."

Thomas Aquinas College describes their new program syllabus as, "*Composed exclusively of the just barely adequate texts that have, for good or for ill, kinda-sorta animated, for the lack of a better word, Western civilization.*"

The announcement comes just days after the University of Notre Dame announced the continuation of their *Mediocre Books* program, which includes books such as *Heaven Is For Real*, as well as Judy Bloom's theological treatise, *Are You There, God? It's Me, Margaret.*

SSPX Vehemently Protesting
Canonization of St. Peter

Members of the Society of St. Pius X have stormed the internet and radio waves in violent protest against the upcoming canonization of Pope Simon Peter I. The backlash was worse than expected by the Holy See, and the protesters have not pulled any punches.

One commentator on popular Tridentine website more-catholicthanthepope.com wrote, "This is the guy who denied Christ *three times* in *one night*, and now they want to *canonize* him? This isn't the way Christ instituted the Church. This man is not an example to me or my fourteen children."

An SSPX blogger accused the former Pope, who was martyred for his faith in the First Century, of liturgical abuses, saying, "Christ was crucified head-upward. That is the pattern He established. Then this Peter guy comes along and decides he wants to be crucified upside-down."

Some have even accused Peter, born Simon, son of John, of heresy in his famous debate with Paul regarding circumcision, while others claim his attitude toward the "circumcision party" was not true heresy but an exaggerated ecumenism.

New Poll Shows 50% of Catholics Disagree with Jesus' Stance on Gay Marriage

A new poll out today shows that about half of Catholics in America still disagree with the Second Person of the Trinity's stance on gay marriage.

The automated poll, commissioned by the USCCB, asked 10,000 Catholics whether or not they agreed with Jesus' objection to gay marriage. Of those polled, half said they disagreed with Jesus' stance because they believed an objection to someone's freedom of choice was unchristian. When one man polled was asked to rectify the apparent disparity between his belief in the inerrancy of God's word with his objection to the inerrancy of God's word in regards to homosexual unions, he asked, "What does inerrancy mean?" Another woman was asked whether she believed Jesus was unchristian in his stance on gay marriage: "Oh you mean *Jesus*, Jesus...like as in Jesus *Christ*," she responded. "I thought you were talking about that nice Mexican man who sits in the back of church with his family. I was gonna say...he doesn't seem like the judgmental type."

Disobedient SSPV Woman Wearing
Shoes in Kitchen

Local member of the Society of St. Pius V, Marisa Conti, reported Tuesday that she planned to wear shoes in the kitchen despite a recent ruling by SSPV and her husband rejecting her request to wear them in the kitchen.

"You know...putting on a pair of shoes before entering the kitchen will most certainly be the single most exhilarating moment of my life. I'm actually scared that, not being used to the feeling of grip against tile, I might actually trip," Conti nervously said as she took her first daring step into the kitchen, awkwardly stumbling across the tiled kitchen floor like a newborn calf. "One small step for an SSPV woman...one giant leap for SSPV!"

Conti's husband, Benjamin Conti, told EOTT that he was "utterly" ashamed of his wife, and blamed recent changes in his wife on her more liberal-minded SSPX girlfriends. "If I told her once, I've told her a million times...get rid of those friends," he said as he cleaned out the sanitary pit privy of their outhouse. "She's not pregnant, and now she's walking around the kitchen with shoes on like some kinda floozy."

Marty Haugen Music to Be Outlawed under New Geneva Convention Resolution

New guidelines set down by the international community during the fifth Geneva Convention this week have extensively defined the basic, spiritual wartime rights of the Church Militant by outlawing all Marty Haugen music used in and around war zones.

What is officially being called *The Geneva Convention Relative to the Protection of Parishioners in Times of Spiritual War* has become the fifth convention establishing the standards on international law for the humanitarian treatment of spiritual war.

"Our new resolution states that all Catholics who are in the process of spiritual warfare are to be treated humanely," said General of the Counsel, Robert Durant, at a press conference earlier this morning. "The following acts are to be henceforth prohibited: Violence to life and person, in particular, cruel treatment and torture by means of being made to listen to "Gather Us In"; outrages upon personal dignity, in particular humiliating and degrading treatment such as asking parishioners to sing along to "We Remember"; and finally, all acts requiring parishioners to listen to said music during the reception of communion."

Pope Francis Declares Homosexuality Obligatory for All Catholics, New York Times Reports

During an interview given while on his airplane, His Holiness Pope Francis declared the new ex-cathedra Catholic dogma that all members of the Catholic Church must become homosexual, *The New York Times* reported.

This declaration is said by *The New York Times* to have sent shock waves through the Catholic world, and delighted the enormously powerful "Gay Lobby," said by *The Times* to control the interior workings of the Holy See.

"If someone is gay and he searches for the Lord and has good will, who am I to judge, and would it not be judgmental for me to not require all Catholics to walk in his footsteps?" the Holy Father reportedly told *The New York Times*. This comes in stark contrast to the words of Pope Benedict XVI, who, according to *The New York Times*, said that, "If someone is gay and he searches for the Lord and has good will, it is the duty of every Catholic to judge him."

An Excited Peter Kreeft Receives
Peter Kreeft Book for Birthday

Citing the fact that almost nothing in the world is better than receiving a Peter Kreeft book as a gift, an enthusiastic Peter Kreeft was reportedly overjoyed at having received one of his own books for his birthday.

According to many of his friends gathered for his birthday party, Kreeft was also given a copy of a manuscript of an upcoming book.

"This is one of the greatest days of my life," Peter Kreeft told friends as he sat around heaps of giftwrapping paper. "Kreeft books are the best. I've written so much good stuff that sometimes I'll be reading a book, thinking, 'darn, this is good stuff,' just to realize that *I'm* the one who wrote it."

Kreeft went on to say that he now had every one of his own books, and that he would now devote the rest of his life to studying and memorizing all the insightful things found in his own books.

At press time, Kreeft was trying to get in touch with his agent to request an autograph.

"This is one of the greatest days of my life," Peter Kreeft told friends as he sat around heaps of giftwrapping paper. "Kreeft books are the best. I've written so much good stuff that sometimes I'll be reading a book, thinking, 'darn, this is good stuff,' just to realize that *I'm* the one who wrote it."

USCCB to Publish Compendium of the Compendium of the Catechism for College Students

It was announced today that the United States Conference of Catholic Bishops will be coming out with their highly anticipated *Compendium of the Compendium of the Catechism of the Catholic Church for College Students* this May.

The abridged version of the compendium will attempt to lessen the page count from 200 pages to a more manageable twenty pages. Other highlights of the *Compendium of the Compendium* will include colored pictures on each page, three pop-out images, and the "Are You Following Me?" section, which will help ensure that the reader has not gotten distracted. One Catholic college student asked what he thought about the upcoming *Compendium of the Compendium* publication responded, "What?"

The following is a sneak preview to some title changes in the new compendium:

Part One: "The Profession of Faith," will be changed to, *"Stuff You Should Probably Know."*

Part Two: "The Celebration of the Christian Mystery," will be changed to, *"Chill... It's Only One Freakin' Hour."*

Part Three: "Life In Christ," will be changed to, *"Do The Exact Opposite Of What You're Doing Now."*

Part Four: "Christian Prayer," will be changed to, *"Just Close Your Eyes And Pretend You're Texting Jesus With Your Brain."*

Catholics for Choice Asks Vatican to
Allow Abortions in Cases of
Rape, Incest, Impending Prom

The pro-choice organization *Catholics for Choice* sent a request to the Vatican today, asking them to ease restrictions on abortions in cases of rape, incest, and impending prom.

The focus of the letter was aimed primarily at the subject of impending, "once in a lifetime" proms that many unfortunate teens are forced to miss due to unplanned and untimely pregnancies. The request, sent by *Catholics for Choice* President, Jon O'Brian, was on behalf of "all those women who have a dream to dream; a dream of a future; a dream of a hot date and a hot dress that, very much like their future, they would like to resist from altering."

Pope Francis to Investigate Roman Curia on TV Show Undercover Boss

Executives from CBS confirmed Wednesday that Chief Executive Officer of *The One, Holy, Catholic, and Apostolic Church,* Pope Francis, would be appearing in this season's finale of the hit television show *Undercover Boss.*

The finale, slated to appear in late May, will feature the Pontiff taking on an alias and fictional backstory as he navigates his way through different parts of the Vatican in an attempt to investigate the inner workings of the Curia. Series creator and producer, Stephen Lambert, told EOTT that it was one of the most difficult episodes he's ever worked on. "Usually it's the CEO of 1-800-FLOWERS or something, so it's typically a lot easier to hide their identity...but when it's the Bishop of Rome, that's when it gets a bit tricky." Lambert went on to say that the episode had some hallmark moments, especially the moment his true identity is revealed. "Everyone is shocked, as expected. But what really shocked *us* most was how many people said, 'Oh, crap,' after the revelation."

SSPX Laity Don't Even Really Need to Be That Condescending, New Study Shows

According to a study out today by the United States Conference of Catholic Bishops, members of the Society of St. Pius X don't actually need to be insufferable, condescending bastards.

"We assumed for decades that Rad Trads acted like arrogant little pricks because they were frustrated at Vatican II reforms," said lead study author Gertrude Stone, adding that most pretentious SSPX members only went completely "apeshit troll" on website comment boxes and internet threads as a means of releasing years of pent up frustration, when all that was scientifically needed was a little prayer time. "The thing is, they might pray, but we also found that ninety-five percent of their prayers consisted of some sort of revenge, as opposed to the more therapeutic and productive prayers such as those of forgiveness."

Stone added that most SSPX members are simply patronizing because of the sadistic enjoyment they get out of riling people up.

"They choose to get under people's skin and to become the defacto party buzzkill not out of choice, but necessity. Buzzkill or killjoy, what have you, is like a drug, and many simply have a very difficult time quitting, not that many have ever tried. Our study shows that quitting being an insufferable, condescending, pretentious little prick of a bastard is a disease. That's the reason why it's harder to quit than cocaine. We need to pray for these people."

ICEL Calls for All-Meme Missal
Translation for Youth Masses

Citing a need for the Church to "reach out to its estranged youth," the International Commission on English in the Liturgy requested, and has already begun intensive work on, an all-meme edition of the Roman Missal.

Representatives from the Commission, unhappy with last year's implementation of the new translation of the Missal, shared their concern that the Church is not "speaking the language of the people."

"Young people are unable to relate to [the Missal's] rigid, academic language," said a spokesperson for the group, "and so we are taking it upon ourselves to bring them closer to the richness of the Catholic Faith through the most modern meme-linguistic-format."

Such meme-characters as "Bad Luck Brian," "The Most Interesting Man in the World," and "Skeptical Black Kid," the new mouthpieces of the Roman Liturgy, would be projected on the bare walls of churches behind the altar, to allow for "full, active participation" of young people during the Sacred Rites.

Head of Newly-Created Congregation for Doctrine of Praise and Worship Urges All Young Believers in House to Wave Hands in Air Like They Just Don't Care

Noting that there appeared to be a scarcity of praise in today's youth, head of the newly-created Congregation of the Doctrine of Praise and Worship (CDPW), Reverend Lil J, has recommended that all the young Catholics in the house "put they hands up, put they hands up, and wave them like they just don't care."

Reverend Lil J, formerly of the Catholic boy band N'Sync With The Word, gave his recommendation at a local Lifeteen Mass, where he also stressed the importance of partying like it was Jesus' birthday, and also making sure that all in attendance understood the importance of the Mass and waving "they hands from side to side."

"JC can't hear you!" Lil J hollered at the crowd moments before the consecration. "I said...JC can't hear you! Louder, y'all. Let me ask you, what good it do to pray if yo hands ain't in the air? How JC gonna notice you? And if you put 'em up, but don't wave 'em, it's like tellin' JC that you need Him, but not enough to put in your own work. Y'all understandin' me now, ain't you? Ha-ha, dat's right."

Peter Jackson Announces Plans for 72-Part Movie Series of *The Silmarillion*

At a press conference today outside his estate in Beverly Hills, acclaimed director Peter Jackson announced his plans to make a seventy-two-film adaptation of J. R. R. Tolkien's *The Silmarillion*. "It was the next logical step after doing *The Lord of the Rings* and *The Hobbit*," Jackson said. "In *The Lord of the Rings*, we took over a thousand pages of novel and adapted it to the big screen in three extremely long films. Then in *The Hobbit,* we took a children's book that's a fraction of the length of *The Lord of the Rings*, and also made it into three extremely long films."

Jackson then unfolded his plan for Tolkien's *The Silmarillion*, which begins with a mythological account of the creation of Middle Earth and culminates in the great battles of the Elves during the First Age. "The first film in the series is set to come out in Summer 2016. Then, every two years from 2018 to 2160, the following installment will be released."

Returning to the original cinematic backgrounds of *The Lord of the Rings* movies, Jackson made an executive decision to save costs for shooting the outdoor scenes, and had his studio purchase the entire island of New Zealand. "In the long run it will cost us a lot less. Plus, now the citizens of New Zealand are the property of our studio, so we get free labor to build sets."

Movie buffs and Tolkien nerds alike are ecstatic over the news, and Jackson, as usual, is enjoying the attention, teasing fans about the contents of some of the seventy-two movies they can look forward to. "Sixteen of the movies will be almost exclusively footage of the elven-folk doing various dances, and I don't want to say much, but *The Silmarillion: Part 49* is subtitled *Gandalf Smokes his Pipe*."

Months after Abolishing "Monsignor" Honor for Priests, Pope Abolishes "Priest" Honor for Seminarians

Months after abolishing the title of "monsignor," Pope Francis has now reportedly eliminated the practice of granting seminarians the title of "priest," a Vatican insider told EOTT this morning from Rome.

According to a report Sunday by the Italian newspaper *La Repubblica*, only single laymen over the age of 65 will from now on be eligible to receive the title of priest. "The title of priest is primarily honorific, and should normally only be granted to laymen as a reward for service to the church, such as having been an usher for more than four decades," Apostolic Nuncio to the United States, Giovanni Martinelli, told EOTT. "Or it should be given as a sign of a unique function a layman has performed in the church, such as being the guy who selects which family will walk the gifts up to the altar."

The title was once granted by a bishop on the recommendation of God. But many have criticized the practice, saying that ordination naturally leads to an "air of careerism in the church."

According to Martinelli, every nuncio across the globe has been asked to write to bishops within their territories to inform them of the pope's decision and to say that those who have already been given the title of priest can keep it; for now.

VATICAN

"EWTN has been a partner with the Holy See for many years, and I am very pleased and excited that this highly respected organization will become a part of the EWTN family of services," said network chairman, Michael P. Warsaw. "Since its founding two-thousand years ago, the Vatican has proven itself to be a valuable source for all things Catholic."

EWTN Acquires Holy See

EWTN Global Catholic Network announced today that it has acquired the Vatican-based Holy See.

"EWTN has been a partner with the Holy See for many years, and I am very pleased and excited that this highly respected organization will become a part of the EWTN family of services," said network chairman, Michael P. Warsaw. "Since its founding two thousand years ago, the Vatican has proven itself to be a valuable source for all things Catholic."

Under the terms of the agreement, no cash will be exchanged between the parties, and EWTN will assume control of all ongoing activities of the Vatican. Host of *The World Over*, Raymond Arroyo, is expected to be named new head of the Congregation for the Doctrine of the Faith.

"Among other impressive accomplishments, the Vatican is the world's largest charitable organization in the world," Arroyo said. "It was founded in 33 A.D. and it's been expanding ever since. I truly believe that this union is a match made in Heaven."

Though the Holy See has long been a player in religion, it has struggled of late with many financial issues. But many analysts are saying that with EWTN's power and influence now backing the Holy See, it should really start becoming a real contender again.

Pope Francis Sneaks out of Vatican at Night in Disguise to Help Poor, Fight Crime

A recent interview with the Papal Alomner Archbishop Konrad Krajewski this week confirmed recent speculations that Pope Francis joins him on his nightly trips into Rome to give alms to the poor.

An inside source at the Vatican told EOTT that "Swiss guards confirmed that the pope has ventured out at night dressed as Batman to meet with homeless men and women, and to fight crime."

"The first time I told him I was going out into the city in the evening, there was the risk that he would want to come with me," Krajewski said in an interview this morning. "And when I did tell him, he merely smiled and ran away to get ready."

Krajewski went on to say that just moments after his discussion with Francis, he witnessed the Holy Father's Pope Mobile, "painted all black," racing out of St. Peter's Square with flames coming out of the back end. "Honestly, though, I don't think the flames were coming out because of how fast the car was, but because it's a 1984 Renault. The thing's about to explode."

The "hands-on project," which involves face-to-face meetings with the homeless and the poor, as well as fist-to-face meetings with adversaries, is managed by the Church's charity in an effort to directly impact the lives of the people of Rome. The new Papal Butler, Roberto Bartone, told EOTT in an interview via Skype earlier today that he did not like Francis leaving the Vatican, and wished he would retire like Benedict. "It's far too dangerous," he said. "Just last week I got very angry at him because of the risks he was taking. I said to him, 'Remember when you left Argentina and were elected? Well, every month since you were elected, I've been taking a weekend holiday… I go to Florence. There's this café on the banks of the Arno. Every fine evening I sit there and order a Fernet-Branca. I have this fantasy that I'll look across the tables and see you there, with a friend, maybe a couple of religious statues. You wouldn't say anything to me, nor me to you, but we'd both know…that you'd made it…that you were happy.'"

Vatican Announces New "Three Strike" Excommunication Policy

The Vatican has announced today that beginning next year, a new three-strike excommunication policy will take effect.

The new three-strike policy would automatically excommunicate anyone found guilty of having committed three mortal sins.

"We are mandating this new policy because we have found that too many Catholics are either committing the same sins over and over again because they know they can simply come to confession right after, or because they simply aren't afraid of the consequences," said the Vatican Chief Confessions and Penance Czar, Father Antonio Sabalette. "Once people know they're just one lustful look at a woman away from eternal damnation without the possibility of Purgatory, we anticipate a strong decline in sinning."

Sabalette went on to tell EOTT that with the new measures to curb sinning, four of the eight remaining functioning confessionals in the United States would be demolished to make room for more banner space.

"This is a good time in the Church. I feel happy knowing that the last remaining priests still hearing confessions in the U.S. will finally have free time on Saturdays from three to four to focus on other things like blogging."

Vatican Unveils New Eucharist Delivery Service

After years of anticipation and speculation, the USCCB's long awaited Eucharist Delivery Service was announced this morning in Washington, D.C.

Using a powerpoint presentation to explain the features, benefits, and user-friendly app of Eucharist Delivery Service (EDS), Cardinal Timothy Dolan of New York praised the revolutionary new means by which parishioners unable or unwilling to go to Mass could now receive communion from the comfort of their homes.

"The Eucharist is indispensable to the spiritual life," Dolan told hundreds gathered for the reveal. "But with so many having to work Sundays or unable to attend Mass due to numerous reasons, they will now be able to receive the spiritual sustenance that only the Eucharist can provide, without having to leave their homes, or miss a game."

The charge for EDS will be a suggested donation of one dollar, which will cover the donation the consumer would've most likely made had they attended Mass, plus gas money for the delivery driver.

SSPX Accepts Vatican Offer to Mutually Mock SSPV

After close to two weeks of intense meetings between the Vatican and the Society of St. Pius X, the two officially agreed to terms regarding the mutual mockery of the sedevacantist group The Society of St. Pius V.

According to the conditions of the agreement, SSPX, as well as its members, in communion with Rome, will now share full rights in the mocking of the schismatic organization, as well as its "freak members."

"This is a great day," said Vatican spokesman Alberto Gallucci. "It is with great pleasure that I can announce that the Vatican and SSPX have found more common ground on which to build. We would like to thank members of SSPV for breaking off of SSPX, without whom this reconciliation could never have happened. We look forward to years of coming together on blogs and pulpits alike to mercilessly offer SSPV mockery and verbal bashing, and we hope that, with both sides finally united, we might be able to further the cause of formal reunification, as well as years of success in going absolutely apeshit on those freaks."

Bitter Old Man Writes Angry Letter
to Vatican Using All Caps

Writing under the pen name "Nerocious," 67-year-old Max Kroeger of Boonville, North Carolina sent an irate letter to the Vatican this week denouncing what he called the "abuse and corruption" inside the Vatican. Kroeger reported this morning that the 12,000-word letter addressed to "TO WHOM IT **MUST** CONCERN" was the fruit of a vigorous and ferocious one-hour writing session he had had the prior evening after finishing the book *Hitler's Pope*.

Father Roberto Abate, who had the privilege of opening the letter, told EOTT that he had never seen such a well-crafted letter in all his years. "It was outstanding," Abate said, still in tears by the fervor that seemed to pour forth from the passionately written letter. "I was moved even before I read its contents. The entire thing was written in caps, which automatically caught my attention and alerted me to the fact that this was a serious matter, and that this man, whoever he was, was extremely furious about the state of the Church." Abate went on to say that the masterfully executed letter, with its flawless use of all caps, as well as a large number of just perfectly positioned bold words that helped to emphasize certain aspects Kroeger believed the Church was lacking, could very well make it to the Holy Father's desk.

"This is what the Pope likes to see. It is not enough to write a letter. You must mean it... You must make it stand out. After all, without capitalized words, bold words, underlined words, and perhaps even highlighted words pointing out phrases that you don't want the reader to overlook, how can you expect anyone to know that you're frustrated?"

Vatican Announces Church Nearly out of Eucharist Host

The Vatican, in communion with all the Catholic churches around the world, announced today that due to a worldwide shortage of Eucharistic bread, only a select number of people are to be allowed the Eucharist at each Mass.

"Not much else we can do until the nuns are able to catch up," said Ronaldo Brevi, head of the Congregation of Near Impossible Situations. "Due to the shortage of Eucharistic bread, which is in part due to the shortage of nuns, we have allotted each parish in the world seven hosts per Sunday. That's one for the priest, and the remaining six will be given out according to lottery, which will take place just before the consecration."

Brevi went on to ask all those with the stain of mortal sin on them to refrain from the Eucharist as they should have been anyway.

"By taking people with mortal sin on them out of the lottery, that will basically only leave about like six people to enter the lottery anyway, so we should be good. In my opinion, this can actually be looked at as a good thing."

Vatican to Build Vatican II Theme Park

Speaking to the press Wednesday afternoon, the Prefect of the Congregation of the Doctrine of Faith announced plans to create the first ever Vatican II theme park.

"We're very thrilled about the opportunities that the theme park will bring to the Church. In particular, we're excited to see how it may become a tool for fostering a culture of open dialogue within a fun and exciting setting," the prefect said, before giving reporters an inside look at one of the rides being developed for the park.

"We have many rides being developed as we speak, but one of my favorites is our state-of-the-art Ferris wheel where Vatican and SSPX officials can sit down and discuss the important issues of Vatican II while going around in circles."

An SSPX spokesman later told EOTT that they reject the premise of the theme park altogether, and that they plan to dissuade their followers from entering, saying, "It is an evil theme park; that is the correct term to describe it...not invalid or illicit, but evil."

Pope Francis Not Sure How to Make Sense of What He Just Said

Speaking to pilgrims during his weekly Wednesday audience yesterday, Pope Francis admitted that he was kind of having a hard time making any kind of sense whatsoever of what he just said.

The Pontiff, who has been known to make off the cuff remarks in the past, told those gathered in St. Peter's Square that what he just said was "admittedly kind of weird."

"I said what?" Francis asked those gathered. "There's no way I just said that. OK, that's just weird. Seriously, what the heck is it with me? Am I trying to change doctrine or something? How am I gonna explain this to my secular friends? Oh boy, I can see their faces now. I bet they're just itching to ask when I'm gonna start allowing divorced gay Catholics to receive communion. This is great...just great. I'm so freaking pissed right now I think I'm gonna go blog about it."

Broke Vatican Forced to Sell Parishioners

Announcing to his flock early this afternoon that the diocese was in financial straits, local bishop Edward Wright told the faithful that, so as to avoid bankruptcy, he was forced to make the difficult decision to sell a number of local Catholics to neighboring Protestant communities.

"We have reached out to our Protestant brethren and they have offered to help," Wright announced in his weekly newsletter. "At the price ranging anywhere from $250 to $500 a parishioner, I believe this is a step in the right direction to fix our financial situation."

Wright mentioned that according to priests in the diocese, there are many Catholics who were bound to leave the Church anyway, "so why not make a buck out of them."

"Those who have shown skepticism to some of the Church's teachings will be first to be sold off. From there we will move on to the non-essentials, or those who do not frequent Mass."

In his conclusion, Wright said that those safe from being sold were those families who have donated "substantial" amounts of money in the past year. In other words, those who have put more than a dollar in the collection basket on a weekly basis.

Vatican Insiders Reveal Holy Father Resigned Because Roman Curia "Too Fabulous"

Sources close to Pope Benedict revealed today that the ultimate reason for his resignation was not his old age, but in fact an inability to keep up with the "fabulousness" of the Roman Curia.

"The Holy Father is a simple man," one source said, "and can't keep up with the non-stop furniture re-arrangements, the hairstyling, or the near-hourly musical numbers he found himself surrounded by in the Vatican."

The source revealed that, in mid-conversation, members of the Roman Curia often break out into song and dance routines "in order to better express their feelings." It was apparently this exuberant, flamboyant lifestyle that the Holy Father felt he could not keep up with in his old age. "I mean, just look at the way he dresses. There's no way he could do mid-air splits in that old cassock. And white is *so* 2010." The source added, "I mean, he did pull out the pink chasuble once or twice a year, but that's not exactly up to speed on the amount of flare expected these days in the Vatican." The source concluded, addressing the tiny dog he was carrying: "Is it, pwincess?"

"The Holy Father is a simple man," one source said, "and can't keep up with the non-stop furniture re-arrangements, the hairstyling, or the near-hourly musical numbers he found himself surrounded by in the Vatican."

USCCB Announces Publication of
New Mad Libs Missal

In hopes of providing the nation's Catholic priests a way to follow the Missal, while at the same time preserving the creative outlet some need to prevent boredom, the USCCB announced today the publication of an all-new *Mad Libs Roman Missal*.

The new Missal, due out next month, allows the presiding priest to insert the adverbs and adjectives he feels best fit the mood of that particular day.

"There's a debate in this country about why so many Catholics aren't attending Mass," said USCCB spokeswoman Margaret Charter. "Some say it's because there's too much ad libbing during the Mass, which turns off more traditional-minded people. Others say it's the complete opposite, and that not enough Masses are ad libbed, turning off more liberal-minded people. I think we've found a good medium with the *Mad Libs Missal*."

Parishioners objecting to the new Missal are being encouraged to take full advantage of this exciting new way to participate in the Mass, and to brush up on their adjectives, possessive nouns, and love for the Lord, Holy Father, (adjective) and Eternal (noun).

EVERYTHING ELSE

"I looked out and saw all these college kids reading text messages on their phones," Conti said. "That's when I knew the Church needed to catch up or risk being left behind, so to speak. So I figured, heck, if they're already on their phones, might just be easier to text them the prompts and they can just text back the responses."

Atheists Sue to Remove Letters
"G," "O," and "D" from Alphabet

The civil liberties organization *American Atheistic People* has sued the U.S. government to remove the letters "G," "O," and "D" from the English alphabet, arguing that the letters «often come together in such an order as to promote a belief in God," its director, Edward Kegin, said Friday. "The letters represent a violation of rights to many atheists around the country, in that the letters are being misused to promote religion."

Some now believe that the lawsuit may eventually be modified so as to also remove the letters "F," "A," "T," "H," "E," and "R."

American Atheists' President, David Goldman, said that the letters are an "offense and no less of an attack on the rights of man than was the inquisition."

In a letter to members of American Atheists on Friday, Silverman wrote, *W- c-n n- l-n--- s--n- by -n- w--c- -s -u- -i---s -n- --- ---ms --- ---mpl-- -n by --li-i-us z--l--s. N- l-n---...n- m---!*

Report: All That Really Matters
Is Having a Good Heart

A new study released today by millions of Catholics and non-Catholics from across the globe shows that having a good heart is more pleasing to God than following the teachings of the Church.

"I'm so happy to say that after close to two thousand years of dogmatism, we have successfully proven that the way into God's heart, and ultimately into Heaven, is not by going to church or confessions, but by being nice," said Hugh Benson, the 48-year-old lapsed Catholic who spearheaded the study. "It's not to say that Catholics who go to Mass cannot go to heaven, but it's that church-goers do tend to become intolerant and consequently, mean. The study proves that it's perhaps easier for a camel to go through the eye of a needle than for someone who is devout to enter the Kingdom of God…or Allah, or Buddha, or Mother Earth."

Benson added that, along with being nice, the study also showed that smiling and never criticizing is "truly the essence of being a Doctor of the Church, here on earth."

"It all comes down to Karma. Jesus did many good things, and yet he died. How does that fit in with Karma? Who knows, perhaps it was because he lost his temper and overturned the tables of the money changers. Perhaps he hurt a couple doves in the process. That's not nice."

Thin Confessional Walls to Be Thinned out More by Advent

Announcing a sweeping new initiative that is to take effect this Advent, USCCB officials announced this week that all confessional walls are to be thinned out to make it more difficult for parishioners in line to not overhear the person presently confessing his or her sins.

"We ask all Catholics in the United States to begin practicing ways to drown out the sound of weeping or concrete words that will inevitably make their way out of the confessional," said USCCB spokesman Bishop Donald Winters. "Plugging your ears, tapping your feet, or humming a hymn has been known to work in the past, but the measures we are taking now to thin out the walls will hopefully make it more difficult. You're going to need to be more creative in your methods starting this Advent."

Winters told EOTT that the reason for the new measure is to keep Catholics on their toes and to allow the faithful an opportunity to work on their focus when in Church.

"Not only will this allow Catholics the amazing chance to practice their meditation, but we hope that this will also give them the opportunity to come together to figure out as one family, one team, just how the heck they can overcome the awkwardness of the moment."

In conclusion, Winters said that this will also hopefully decrease the number or gravity of sins Catholics are committing, knowing full well that everyone is probably going to be able to overhear their most private sins.

New Text Message Mass All the Rage
at Gonzaga University

Expressing sadness for the lack of attention from parishioners during Sunday Masses, Gonzaga University chaplain Fr. John Conti has recently instituted an all new "Text-Message-Only Mass."

The Gonzaga graduate, who just celebrated his 15th anniversary as a priest, told reporters that the idea came to him as he sat listening to the deacon read the epistle. "I looked out and saw all these college kids reading text messages on their phones," Conti said. "That's when I knew the Church needed to catch up or risk being left behind, so to speak. So I figured, heck, if they're already on their phones, might just be easier to text them the prompts and they can just text back the responses."

Conti went on to say that people can think of the new approach to the Mass as a "Novus Ordo Low Mass," in that it's quiet throughout the Mass, and that the text messages are in the vernacular rather than Latin.

20-year-old Gonzaga junior Jane Douglas told EOTT that the Text-Message-Only Mass has made her enjoy going to Mass again. "It's sorta awesome now. Last Sunday I was texting my boyfriend and I got this text that was all like 'Th Lord b W u,' and I was all texting back like, 'n w ur spirit ;),' and then I went back to texting my boyfriend, and we decided we'd just go pick up my roommate Sarah and *then* go to the BYOB. I guess it's just kinda cool to know you don't have to leave your social life just cause you're at church." Conti says that if it weren't for the distribution of the Eucharist, he would be happy to have the Mass go completely virtual; "I like to call it 'e-fellowship.'"

Self-Proclaimed Thomist Admits He
Knows Nothing of Thomas Aquinas

It was reported this week that Gonzaga University grad and self-proclaimed Thomist Stephen Hillers knows virtually nothing about the works of St. Thomas Aquinas.

Hillers, well known for beginning his sentences with the words, "Well, according to Thomas..." came clean to friends late Tuesday night when he revealed that he did, in fact, know nothing about the *Summa Theologica*, and that he had never even heard of the *Summa Contra Gentiles* until that very night.

"We always knew he was full of it," a friend of Hillers said. "But on Tuesday, when Steve said that according to Thomas, the biggest human temptation was to settle for too little...that was too much. I called him out on it."

Hillers has since apologized to his friends, saying that he never meant to mislead anyone. "Really, I didn't. I never meant Thomas Aquinas. I meant 'Thomist' as in a student of Thomas Merton. Ever heard of him?" Hillers said he intends to begin reading *Seven Story Mountain* this fall.

"Really, I didn't. I never meant Thomas Aquinas. I meant 'Thomist' as in a student of Thomas Merton. Ever heard of him?"

Thousands Expected to Ring in the Solemnity of Mary Mother of God in Times Square

Final preparations are underway in New York City this morning as hundreds of volunteers work to transform Times Square into party central in anticipation for tonight's countdown to the Solemnity of Mary, Mother of God.

In the annual event celebrating the Blessed Virgin Mary's divine motherhood to Jesus Christ, thousands are again expected to pack the streets of Times Square to watch the ball drop, ushering in another feast. "We're all very excited for this year's countdown," Times Square Director of Solemnity Festivities, Candice O'Conner, told EOTT. "It's amazing, the electricity and Catholic fervor that you feel once the ball begins to drop. Then when it drops and everyone exchanges kisses of peace and says prayers of thanksgiving... Oh, it's a sight to behold."

New York's own Catholic rap sensation Fr. Stan Fortuna is scheduled to take the stage at 10:45 p.m., followed by a chastity seminar by Jason Evert, ending just minutes before the Waterford Crystal Button is pressed, prompting the descent of the Theotokos Ball.

Ancient Manuscript Reveals Adam Had
Midlife Crisis at Age 452

A recently discovered piece of papyrus unearthed by a Tel Aviv University researcher has revealed that Adam, the Old Testament patriarch who is said to have lived for 930 years, may have suffered a severe midlife crisis at the age of 452.

Tel Aviv University professor Benyamin Zimmermann says he has found an ancient papyrus fragment that appears to indicate that Adam showed symptoms of a midlife crisis, including a portion that mentions that he may have purchased a fast and flashy camel. The portion of the manuscript that is drawing attention reads,

"So when Adam saw that his life's span may have been more than halfway over, and that much of the grey had overtaken his head, he saw a camel of much speed and it brought delight to his eyes. Desiring, therefore, to make use of it, that he may take to the open desert, he didst purchase the camel and ride; and he also, seeing the grey that had overtaken his head, took unto himself fists of pomegranate with which, after crushing into paste, he didst smear upon his head to change the color. And upon seeing all this, he was pleased, but Eve, seeing the same, was very much displeased."

"This is obviously a remarkable find," Zimmermann told EOTT via Skype this morning. "That even the first man struggled with symptoms of a crisis triggered by transitions experienced in the later years of life, called andropause or menopause, is amazing. We know by the accounts in Genesis, that because of the first sin, woman's pangs during childbirth would increase, and I think we can now safely assume that man, because of that same sin, would have to suffer the reality that he would grow old and lose his hair and consequently have to compensate in other ways.

Man on Catholic Match Finally
Ready to Message Kristin-51053

31-year-old Chuck-50012 has finally finished writing his message to Kristin-51053 after one month and seventeen revisions, his friends are now reporting. The web developer, who celebrated his fifth anniversary on Catholic Match last week, has been working, tirelessly, to write the perfect message. "I don't usually spend this much time on a message," Chuck-50012 said. "Usually I just write a couple lines, 'Hey, how are you?' 'So you live in such-and-such place?' 'I've always wanted to visit,' blah, blah, blah, and then message bomb it to twenty, thirty girls and hope for a response. But there's something about this Kristin-51053 girl."

Friends of Chuck-50012 say that he became smitten with Kristin-51053 the moment he noticed that she had viewed his profile. "I remember he leaned back in his chair and started making this 'ding, ding, ding' kinda slot machine noise and said that he had 'a winner,'" one friend reflected. Kristin-51053, Chuck-50012 believes, has all the qualities he has searched for in a court-worthy girl.

"She's real pretty, in that homeschool kinda way. She lives in Denver, and I hear they're pretty orthodox out there. She's a governess like one of those Jane Austen characters...and one of the three grainy pictures on her profile is of her wearing a mantilla. And on a coincidental, and dare I say 'providential' note, her favorite book in the Bible is John, which just so happens to be my middle name."

Chuck-50012 has graciously provided the message that he will be sending Kristin-51053 for review.

Hey Kristin,

What's up? Doing good? I noticed that you checked me out on the site a few weeks a ago. Flattered. ;) I would've written earlier but I've been sooooo busy with work. You know how it is. Anyhow, just wanted to right and let you know taht I enjoyed you're profile. So I noticed in you're profile that your quarter German. Me too. My dad's full German and my mom's a quarter. "Achtung!" as they used to say, Haha...joking. Seriously though, that Holocaust thing was a fiasco, huh? Sucks, if you ask me. You have any thoughts about what happened? So...Denver, huh? I hear the city's beautiful. I bet you fit in just perfectly out there. :) I've always wanted to visit, but hadn't had a reason till now. Anyway, hope to ehar from you soon. Let me know when's best for you and perhaps I can fly down for the weekend or something.

Chuck

p.s. Governess? Impressive. Is that like those nanny jobs that girls did in the olden days, or is it like your a female governer or something.

Chuck-50012 Still Desperately Awaiting Response from Kristin-51053 on Catholic Match

After drawing international fame last November for his heart-felt message to fellow Catholic Match member Kristin-51053, Chuck-50012 has expressed disappointment to friends and family after not receiving a response for over four months now. The 31-year-old California-based web developer told EOTT that since writing Kristin-51053 he has spent endless hours saying novenas to St. Raphael.

"I must've said hundreds of novenas by now, and still 'K' hasn't written me back," Chuck-50012 said, despondently. "I just don't get it, you know? I mean, after she didn't write me the first week, I thought she was just playing hard to get. Then, after the first *month*, I honestly began to get worried. I thought something may've happened to her. I mean, what reason would she have not to write me back, you know? We have so much in common...both being Catholic and all."

Friends of Chuck-50012 told EOTT that after not receiving a response for a few months he abandoned prayers to St. Raphael (Patron Saint of Singles) and began praying, desperately, to St. Jude (Patron Saint of Lost Causes). "Yeah, he was pretty down and out for a while," longtime friend Chris Ashworth said. "He seems to be getting better now, though. Good thing, too. It was beginning to get kinda weird there for a while...you know, being as how he was obsessed with a girl he had never met before. It *is* over, right?"

Chuck-50012 says that he's been working on a new profile to catch his "damsel's" attention, which he plans to unveil next week. "I'm really excited about next Monday. I have a new profile, new picture. I gotta say I'm super psyched about the new profile pic... I got the whole well-dressed, yet humble, pious, and discerning Italian-American Catholic, leaning-carelessly-against-a-wall kinda thing going on in my new picture. Should be a hit."

Chuck-50012 has graciously provided Eye of the Tiber with a sneak peek at his updated profile.

My Introduction: I was born and raised in San Luis Obispo. For those of you who don't speak Mexican, the the name of the town is translated into English as *saint* luis obispo, after the saint. Love it here. love my church "corpus Cristi" which again is translated from the Mexican meaning "the corpus of christi."

My Ideal Match: Kristin-50153

My Faith: Means so much to me that ive spent the past five years on cathlic match trying to find a good catholic woman to marry and one day God willing bare my children. I love adoration and I love, quite possibly, one ms. (sooner or later "mrs.?") somebody from denver, ehim (cough) Kristin 51053??? ;)

My Favorite Saints: Not St. Rapheal. Maybe St. Jude. We'll see.

Nun Trampled near Scapular Section During "O'Brien's Church Supplies" Black Friday Sale

An O'Brien's Church Supplies shopper was injured earlier today after an out of control mob of frenzied shoppers smashed through the Biloxi store's front doors and trampled her, police said.

The Black Friday stampede plunged the religious goods store into chaos as hundreds of people desperately tried to get their hands on the newly-released Sevenfold Scapular, knocking several employees to the ground and sending others scurrying atop statues to avoid the horde. When the chaos finally ended, 57-year-old Sister Angelica Bettington was injured with a cracked rib and a lacerated spleen.

"She fell over as she tried to get a scapular and then was trampled," said O'Brien's Church Supplies worker Tim Williams. "I haven't seen anything this bad since '98 when the new Credit Card Rosary hit the shelves." 34-year-old Bill Radley, who was looking for a "cheap-looking" cross made of wood from Bethlehem, said that he was temporarily knocked unconscious in the stampede. "When I awoke, I noticed that my cross was broken in half. I still got it because it's made of some sort of olive wood from Bethlehem. That's where Jesus was born, so it must be really powerful. Well worth it." Bettington said that even though all but two of the scapular folds were torn apart in the melee, she was just happy they were the brown and green folds. "Those are the best two anyway, right?"

Report: Jesus Spoke with Spectacular British Accent

A recently discovered DVD found in the attic of the Williams family last night has shed light on the language and accent used by the Son of God while on earth, the Lansing family is reporting this morning.

After close to 2,000 years, the mystery of Jesus' dialect and accent was answered after the Williams family's stunning find while watching a DVD of the 1977 television miniseries *Jesus of Nazareth* produced by the BBC. The two-DVD set, which many in the Williams family believed was "lost forever," showed Jesus of Nazareth speaking in English, a shocking revelation to many who long believed he spoke Aramaic.

"We simply couldn't believe our ears," Jan Williams, 54, reported to EOTT this morning. "I remember, Jesus finally appears in the movie, ready to be baptized by John the Baptist, and John says something like, 'It is I who needs to be baptized by you, and yet, you come to me.' Then Jesus says, 'Let it be so...we must fulfill all righteousness' in the most spectacular British accent." 19-year-old Wendy Williams reported that his British accent was not only "stirring," but that it also contained the dramatic inflection and timing of a "wonderful" stage actor. "It was as though you were listening to the renowned British actor Robert Powell."

At press time, biblical scholars from around the globe are investigating reports that Jesus yelled a lot, and that he did not bleed as much as portrayed in *The Passion of the Christ*.

Replica of Shroud of Turin Replica on Display in Wilmington, Delaware

A replica of the replica of the Shroud of Turin, the hand-painted copy of the replica of the shroud believed to have been wrapped around Jesus after his death, went on display today in Wilmington, Delaware.

"It's amazing to look at," Fr. Jerome Franklin of St. Matthew Catholic Church said. "I mean the people, not the Shroud. It's amazing to just look out at all these Catholics come to venerate a replica of a replica. It's kinda weird, actually." Franklin went on to tell EOTT that, although he "kind of" felt guilty about charging parishioners the $10 admission fee to look at the replica of the replica, he planned to use the money St. Matthew's made to bring the actual replica of the Shroud sometime in the future. "I feel so, so blessed right now!" parishioner Roberta Thomas said as she kissed and touched the relic with a variety of medals and rosaries. "Look...I think some of the paint got on my hands!" At press time, some parishioners were taking pictures of the replica of the replica of the Shroud of Turin to place in their homes.

Man May Have Accidentally Skipped Bead; Begins Decade over Again

After having lost himself in a daydream while saying the rosary earlier this morning, 34-year-old Bridgeport resident Luke Spencer awoke unsure of whether his thumb may have accidentally skipped a couple beads while simultaneously saying his Rosary and dreaming about Japanese snow monkeys bathing in the hot springs of the mountainous region of Nagano, Japan.

"At least I know what decade I'm on," Spencer told EOTT as he tightly gripped the bead he was currently on so as not to lose his place for the fifth time this rosary. "The last thing I remember was meditating on the resurrection, and thinking about Easter Sunday and the Easter Bunny. That led me to bunnies, which led me to my childhood when I'd eat Animal Crackers. The rabbits and monkeys were my favorite, so I began to think about monkeys and, in particular, the Japanese snow monkeys who keep warm in hot springs." Spencer went on to say that although it usually takes him approximately twenty minutes to say a Rosary, he was now moving on to his second hour and still on his first decade.

At press time, Spencer was questioning whether he had said a Hail Mary on the bead he was fingering when this interview began, or whether *that* was the next bead up.

Man with Bullhorn at Catholic Convention Converts Half of Attendees with Stirring Condemnations

More than 1,000 Catholics have been converted away from the Whore of Babylon and into the Baptist church after stirring condemnations made by zealous, bullhorn-wielding Baptist Brock Johnson at this year's Anaheim Catholic Convention, attendees are reporting.

The conversions, which came at the heels of a flurry of condemnations against the Whore of Babylon, were said to be so numerous and passionate that every last one of those converted were finally, truly baptized in the blood of the Lamb that very day.

"Oh yeah, I was on my way in to hear Scott Hahn do some kinda talk about worshiping Mary or praying to statues when I passed this fat, sweaty guy condemning us," said once-Catholic Robby Marshal. "It was that moment that I was converted and made clean by the blood of the Almighty."

Marshal went on to say that there was something about the man's zeal and ear piercing rebukes that drew his attention.

"Save for the fact that the man was white and fat and had ketchup stains on his shirt, the man reminded me of a kind of modern day John the Baptist."

Area Catholic Offended by the Phrase "Merry Christmas"

Local Catholic and Liturgical stickler Gerry Brownstone was offended earlier today when leaving his local Food-Mart, after the greeter wished him a "Merry Christmas."

"Who does that guy think he is, saying that to me?" Brownstone said. "Advent has barely begun. The Liturgical Calendar has a Christmas season, you ignoramus, and it begins *after* the Feast of the Nativity, not a month *before*."

A visibly irritated Brownstone continued, "I don't wish you a Blessed Pentecost the week before the Ascension, do I? Grow up." When asked what he preferred as an Advent salutation, Brownstone answered: "I don't know. Maybe something about the Season of Advent, like 'Advent's Greetings,' or something about the holiness of the days that are coming, like 'Happy Holidays.' Either of those would be liturgically more acceptable."

He concluded his tirade, "It's like there's a war on Advent out there."

"Who does that guy think he is, saying that to me?" Brownstone said. "Advent has barely begun. The Liturgical Calendar has a Christmas season, you ignoramus, and it begins *after* the Feast of the Nativity, not a month *before*."

Local Catholic Gazing at Ressurexifix Not Sure Whether to Mourn or Rejoice

According to sources close to local Catholic Kayla Watkins, the 27-year-old woman is completely confused as to whether she ought to be mourning or celebrating as she gazes at the new ressurexifix at her parish.

The new cross with resurrected Christ hovering in front has reportedly caused Watkins to stray from her prayers for a fifth time in ten minutes as she ponders whether she should be pondering the death or resurrection of her Lord.

"At first, I just knelt there wondering what to think," Watkins told EOTT after a futile fifteen minutes in front of the ressurexifix. "In the end, I decided not to ponder the resurrection *or* crucifixion, but rather, the monstrosity of the new cross."

Watkins also said that she planned on approaching her pastor regarding the new ressurexifix, but that he was preoccupied sculpting his take on the Pieta, with the Virgin Mary holding Christ's resurrected body in her arms as she weeps.

Christian Groups Protest To "Keep the Christ in X-Men"

Decrying the recent secularization of the comic book industry, Christian groups across the nation are joining forces to defend traditional values in the "War on X-Men."

"First the God-given charisms of the X-Men are explained by a bogus evolutionary theory of 'mutation,' now Christ is completely taken out of the picture," said a spokesperson at a local demonstration in front of "Comics n' Whatnot." "The next thing you know, we won't be able to send our kids to school wearing Wolverine t-shirts or be able to express our beliefs at all."

When asked why this was the issue being protested and not the more common phrase "Xmas," the spokesman answered, "Well the X in Xmas comes from the Greek letter Chi, the first letter in Christos. Protesting that would just be silly."

Two-Year-Old Boy Named Lefebvre Being Extremely Disobedient to Father

Citing his son's refusal to adhere to any of his warnings, Robert Kosheta, once proud father of local two-year-old Lefebvre Kosheta, reported today that he was extremely disappointed with his son's stubborn refusal to simply listen to him.

After many months of Lefebvre's ever-growing temper and obstinate resistance to anything his father said, Robert Kosheta told EOTT that Lefebvre was officially grounded, and would not be able to play with any of his brothers or sisters.

"He's still allowed to play with his toys," a worn out Robert Kosheta said. "I can't take those away from him...but I can ground him until he learns to give in a bit. It's not even that he refused to listen that really frustrated me, but that he decided to take it upon himself to make four of the neighborhood kids his brothers without my approval. I'm encouraging the rest of my children to stay away from him and these other kids until the matter is resolved."

At press time, one of Lefebvre's new brothers, little Clarence Kelly, had broken away from Lefebvre's new family, splintering the Kosheta family even more.

Catholic Blog Reader Patiently Waiting for Opportunity to Lambast Someone on Thread

Catholic troll Phillip Karabin, writing under the handle *P90X-celsisDeo,* has been patiently scouring the internet looking to passionately defend everything he holds dear, his friends are reporting.

Sitting at his desk in his mother's basement for the past seven hours, Karabin has settled on a Catholic Answers forum thread titled, *Are Altar-Girls Allowed by the Church?*

"This one's right up my alley," Karabin reportedly told his friends. "Now we wait..." he said, leaning back in his chair and rubbing his hands together before placing them behind his head.

"It's all he does," lifelong friend Brian Reyes told EOTT. "He'll just sit there with his notes...old zingers and good comeback lines he's used on other people, and he'll just wait and wait and wait until someone says the wrong thing. The man's like a freaking sniper."

At press time, Reyes was in the process of writing a 3,000 word, scathing condemnation of the post-conciliar era, citing events chronicled on the news site *Eye of the Tiber* to prove his point.

Four Jesuit Missionaries Dead after
Battle with Portuguese Colonists

Hundreds of Guarani tribe members, including four Jesuit missionaries, were slain early this week when their Mission, located atop the perilous Iguazu Falls on the boundaries of Argentina and Brazil, was attacked by a coalition of Spanish and Portuguese colonists. The Mission's land, once under the protection of the Spanish, had been reapportioned according to a treaty signed last month, essentially transferring the land to the Portuguese.

Cardinal Altamirano, who oversees the Mission territories, came to the decision two weeks ago to abandon the Mission. He told EOTT that the four Jesuits who helped convert the indigenous people had not only feared a Portuguese invasion, but also feared that the Portuguese colonists would make slaves of the Guarani. "I told [the Guarani] they must leave the Mission. I said that they were to submit to the will of God. They, in response, said that it was the will of God that they came out of the jungle and build the Mission, and they did not understand why God had changed his mind. Then they stormed off, and I knew then that they were going to fight."

Reports have now surfaced alleging that at least some of the men who fought with the Guarani may indeed have been the Jesuits themselves. Altamirano confirmed to EOTT that some of the members of the Jesuit Order had fought alongside the Guarani, adding that the head of the Order in Iguazu Falls, Father Gabriel, had not participated in the bloodshed, but rather, had made a dramatic Eucharistic procession, amidst gunfire and breathtaking music, with the women and children of the village before all, including Gabriel, were eventually gunned down.

"Fr. Gabriel did not want to fight," a half-naked little indigenous boy told EOTT. "He told Brother Rodrigo that if might was right, then love had no place in the world. He said like this, he said, 'It might be so. It might be so. But I don't have the strength to live in a world like that, Rodrigo.'"

Brother Rodrigo also died in the battle, with one witness saying that Rodrigo, who chose to fight rather than take part in the procession, died staring almost longingly at Father Gabriel, as if to say, "We both die now, but oh, how I now yearn to have died like you."

In response to the massacre, Altamirano text messaged Portuguese Governor, Don Hontar, asking whether [Hontar] had the effrontery to tell him that the slaughter was necessary. Hontar in response sent a reply informing Altamirano that the both of them must live in the world, and that the world is thus. Altamirano reportedly replied that thus had they made the world; thus had he himself made it.

At press time, Altamirano had written an email to the Pope covering the events that transpired at the Iguazu Falls, reading, "Holiness, now your priests are dead, and I am left alive. But in truth it is I who am dead, and they who live. For as always, your Holiness, the spirit of the dead will survive in the memory of the living."

Pastor Announces Winner of Third Annual
Most Irrelevant Parishioner Award

Last night Samuel Cummings was awarded this year's Most Irrelevant Parishioner of the Year Award at St. Mary Magdalene Parish.

Cummings, who had been nominated for the award for three consecutive years, was finally given the prestigious award for his work in Gum Chewing and Overall Spiritual Apathy.

Runner up, Tobias Garner, told EOTT that he was proud of Cummings, saying that he truly deserved the award for his work in Not Paying Attention or Giving a Crap at All about Anything, but His Fantasy Football Team.

"Especially after last year's snub, this was definitely redemption. He only attended maybe four or five Masses last year, and spent most of the time making last minute adjustments to his fantasy team."

The president of the nominating committee, Candice Danza, said last year that Cummings had not been nominated due to the fact that although he spent most of his time on his phone, the fact that he made it to several Masses during football season excluded him from the nomination, especially with much stronger contenders for the award at the time.

"But this year Cummings came strong," Danza said. "Mr. Cummings won not only the coveted Most Irrelevant Parishioner of the Year Award, but racked up three other awards; Outstanding

Performance for a Father Setting a Bad Example, Business Man Pretending He's Getting a Very Important Call and Not Returning to His Seat until Communion, and Best Lazy Costuming for his work in the Christmas Mass where he wore shorts, a tank top, and flip flops."

Chicago School Board Bans
Crosses and Lowercase T's

In the midst of the political firestorm regarding Montgomery Elementary School student Adrian Townsend's right to wear a cross necklace, the Chicago School Board today announced that crosses, crucifixes, and lowercase T's would be banned in all public schools in the Chicago Unified School District.

"We feel that things such as the cross may be offensive to those students who have no religious affiliation," President of the Chicago School Board, Jennifer Adams, told the press. "But not only crosses, but also things that may resemble them. We've had a complaint from one concerned parent who said that her son had come home after a day of practicing the lowercase 't' telling her that Jesus had died for her sins."

A spokesman for the mother says that it now takes her son much longer to read a sentence, since he stops to kiss every "t" and to utter the words "My Lord and my God," before continuing.

"We feel that things such as the cross may be offensive to those students who have no religious affiliation," President of the Chicago School Board, Jennifer Adams, told the press. "But not only crosses, but also things that may resemble them. We've had a complaint from one concerned parent who said that her son had come home after a day of practicing the lowercase 't' telling her that Jesus had died for her sins."

New "Crucifix for Her" Product Goes on Sale Just in Time for Christmas

For centuries, overly masculine crucifixes have dominated the Catholic market, but one company is set to change that by unveiling their all-new line of crucifixes made "just for her."

The product description reads, *Crucifix For Her has an elegant design—just for Her! It features a thin vertical beam designed to fit a woman's hand as she prays. Deeply sensational, totally feminine, and as contemporary as you are, this crucifix is never afraid to be Glam.*

Product designer Donald Clow told EOTT this morning that he wasn't originally looking to revolutionize the crucifix industry; just the way women pray. "Let's just be honest… Catholic women like to take care of themselves spiritually as well as physically. So we've created a crucifix that not only saves them spiritually, but physically. Gone are the days when a woman needs to leave the adoration chapel to reapply her makeup. Now they can simply flip out the foldout mirror attached to the crucifix. I guess you can call this the Swiss Army crucifix for women. And if you get the upgraded version, you'll be treated to a crucifix with time-released deodorant spray available in four fragrances, as well as a twist off bottom that opens up to reveal your favorite shade of lipstick. Now that's what I call being saved."

Diocese of Fairbanks, Arkansas to Evangelize Modern World by Obtaining an Email Address

Citing a need to "engage the modern world" and "reach out to the estranged youth of America," the Office of Evangelization for the Catholic Diocese of Fairbanks, Arkansas faxed a report to the Associated Press this morning confirming plans that the Diocese will soon be obtaining an email address.

"Once our modem is hooked up, we will be able to take part in the world wide webs," a secretary told EOTT in a letter mailed last week, "and access information in the blink of an eye." The Diocese is hoping that FairbanksDiocese@yahoo.com is not taken, but is willing to settle for FairbanksDiocese2013@yahoo.com.

17-Year-Old Homeschool Boy Figures out Trinity While Mother Combs His Hair

According to the Brandt family moments ago, 17-year-old homeschooler Jake Brandt has solved the greatest mystery known to man. Brandt, who had just gotten out of the shower, reportedly worked out and solved the mystery of the Holy Trinity while his mother, Cherry Brandt, worked furiously to comb down a few stubborn hairs on the back of his head.

"Funny thing is, he's not even the smartest kid on the block," Cherry Brandt told EOTT. "The Jacobs down the street also homeschool, and their son, Nathan, last week was able to make sense of an entire G.K. Chesterton article after just one read through."

Cherry Brandt credits her son's intelligence on the power of prayer, as well as the importance of not allowing him to go near "that sorry excuse for a Catholic school down the road."

Mars Curiosity Rover Successfully
Reaches Jesuit Seminary

NASA announced Tuesday that its 2.5 billion dollar Mars Curiosity Rover has successfully touched down in the Jesuit Seminary in Berkeley.

For close to a decade, the Church and NASA alike have been fascinated with the possibility that the Jesuit seminary might at one time have contained the ingredients needed to support a religious community. The Rover has already begun to send back images to the NASA headquarters in Houston, one of which, researchers believe, appear to be a pair of leather pants.

Report: Most of the Sins You've Ever Confessed Were Not Forgiven Because the Priest Used the Wrong Formula of Absolution

A report released today by the Congregation for the Doctrine of Faith has revealed that most, if not all, of the sins you've ever confessed in your lifetime were never actually forgiven due to the use of improper absolution.

According to the seventy-six-page report, which took into account forgotten or neglected words, as well as coughs and sneezes during absolution, which clearly negates and supersedes the priest's intent to absolve, almost every single confession you've ever made was invalid, and thus, has left you in the state of mortal sin, and just one little accident away from eternal damnation, wherein you will spend the rest of eternity weeping and gnashing your teeth in the fires of Gehenna.

"It definitely sucks," said author of the report, Monsignor Edwardo Totti. "But it is what it is. We are now petitioning the Pope to have three priests in each confessional, so that all three might recite the formula of absolution in unison, giving you better odds of being forgiven."

At press time, His Holiness had rejected the petition, but had agreed to allow speakers in the confessional, that all might hear your sins as well as the priest's absolution, thereby ensuring better odds that someone will catch an invalid absolution.

New Line of Sleek, Sexy, Ankle-Length Jean Jumpers Stirs up Controversy at 2014 Homeschool Fashion Show

Renowned homeschool fashion designer Mary Elisabeth O'Conner kicked off this year's Homeschool Fashion Show, unveiling her new line of sleek and racy ankle-length jean jumpers. The event, which also featured many other star-studded designers and their lines of long, white undershirts and black clogs, has come under scrutiny from the Homeschool Society of Virginia, whose president recently called on homeschool mothers to ban the O'Conner line.

O'Conner's line of ankle-length jean jumpers, called *The Billy Jean Jumper Is Not My Lover* line, has been advertised in traditional Catholic circles around the country with the tagline, "Ankle Is the New Black."

"The fact is that the O'Conner line is lewd, shocking, and indecent," Homeschool Society of America President, Teresa Therese Bryant, told the press. "The line shows far too much ankle. Ms. O'Conner says that this year ankle is in... Next year she'll say it's all about the lower calf. Where does it stop?"

But *The Billy Jean Jumper Is Not My Lover* was not the only line turning heads this year. Legendary homeschool designer Margret Mary shocked crowds after debuting her suggestive and naughty line of long, white undershirts that are worn beneath jumpers, many of which expose close to half an inch of skin below the neck.

Report: It's Seriously Not OK to Presume You Can Just Hold My Hand during Our Father

Emphasizing just how weird and awkward it is when you just straight up reach out and hold my hand during the Our Father even though I've never met you, a new study released by me today confirmed that you should never presume I want you touching me.

The study took in many factors, including the fact that you're a woman and I'm a happily married man, and the fact that you've been sweating profusely ever since you sat down next to me, and that the last thing I want is your surplus of sweat on my perfectly dry hands.

And another thing, while I'm at it, the study went on to reveal; don't even come at me with that whole "fellowship" crap. Christ said, "wherever two or more are gathered in my name, there am I." He didn't make us holding hands a prerequisite for fellowship.

The study concluded, revealing that although you should never ever presume you can hold my hand, that if I violently cough into my palms to direct your hand from coming anywhere near mine, but you still go for it, come germs or cold, you can go ahead and hold it. I won't like it, but your persistence is admirable. You deserve it. But don't push your luck cause I'm not raising my hands at the Doxology. Unless you're stronger than me.

Landmark Win for Individuals Who Experience and Act upon an Exclusive or Predominant Attraction toward Persons of the Same Sex

In a landmark win for thousands of people across America who suffer with and act upon homosexual tendencies, the U.S. Supreme Court yesterday ruled that the Defense of Marriage Act (DOMA) was unconstitutional.

The ruling came as welcome news to hundreds of people gathered outside the Supreme Court who may or may not have recently acted upon intrinsically evil homosexual acts that are contrary to the natural law.

"I just can't believe the day when I can marry my life-partner is almost here," said gay rights activist Jonathan Turner who was just then in the process of being called to fulfill God's will in his life and to unite to the sacrifice of the Lord's Cross the difficulties he was encountering from his condition. 25-year-old Jade Stephans who traveled from San Francisco, and was being called by God to be strengthened by the virtues of self-mastery that teach her inner freedom and at times, by the support of disinterested friendship, by prayer and sacramental grace, so that she could gradually and resolutely approach Christian perfection, told reporters that she was overwhelmed by the decision. "I've prayed and prayed for so many years for this day. This is what God wants. I'm certain of it."

Bombing of St. Augustine High School
Traced to Manicheans

Police officials reported that their investigation following last week's tragic bombing of St. Augustine Academy for Boys has led them to three possible suspects, members of an underground Manichean ring of terrorists in the Nashville area.

"After the bombing, in which six boys and one Augustinian priest were injured," said the Commissioner, "there was a flood of speculation about who would have the heart to commit such an awful act, and who would be holding a grudge this ugly against the Augustinians." After doing their research, which included browsing through the "Augustinians" page on the old Catholic Encyclopedia found on Newadvent.org, the team of investigators began to consider the possibility that this was more than a random act of violence, but could indeed be the result of a centuries-old feud.

"St. Augustine converted from the Manichean religion, and attacked many of its teachings in his subsequent writings," continued the Commissioner. "It is not impossible that this bombing was an act of revenge."

At press time, Manichean groups were protesting at the courthouse, carrying signs reading, "We are a religion of peace."

Berkeley Sophomore Anxiously Considering Coming out of Closet to Reveal He's Opposed to Gay Marriage

University of California, Berkeley student Emanuel Ramsey revealed to EOTT today that he was extremely nervous about possibly coming out of the closet to friends and fellow classmates about his opposition to gay marriage.

The 20-year-old sophomore reported that he always felt like something was different about himself, saying that he first felt the "burning desire" to stand up against gay marriage when he was just a little boy.

"My friend's parents were lesbians," Ramsey said. "I remember going to his house to play, and thinking all I wanted was to just leave...to just go home to witness the tender, heterosexual love of my mother and father...but I felt so ashamed."

Ramsey, who has toyed with the idea of coming out of the closet for some years now, went on to say that growing up in Berkeley, he always felt that he would be ridiculed and picked on if he ever came out against gay marriage. "Look...I'm scared of disappointing my friends, my peers, and even some people at my parish...but the fact is that I'm more afraid of continuing to disappoint *myself*. I've been living a lie and I can't take it anymore. I'm tired of hiding who I really am."

At press time, Ramsey had taken out an old, dusty photo of Archbishop Salvatore Cordileone hiding in his sock drawer, longing for the day he can finally, proudly put it up in his dorm room.

Progressive Catholic School Encouraging Students to Create Their Own Version of Catholicism

Noting that the majority of Catholic high schools in the U.S. were not really that Catholic to begin with, principal of a new progressive Catholic high school in San Diego, California Thomas Shelton told the media this morning that he hopes his new create-it-yourself Catholic curriculum will resonate with students.

"I've worked in so many so-called Catholic high schools in my time," Shelton reported from his office at St. Hollinday Academy. "Seriously, most teachers were just making crap up as they went along anyway, so I thought, 'heck, why even pretend anymore?' You wanna believe everyone goes to heaven? Fine by me. Wanna believe the Church was the instigator behind the inquisition and crusades? Go ahead. Hell, even the saint our academy was named after was made up. No joke…look it up."

Shelton went on to say that the experiment is expected to draw students from other religions looking for more flexible alternatives to strict dogma.

"The only issue we've run into in our test studies was a student whose created version of Catholicism just so happened to be in complete harmony with the teachings of the Magisterium of the Catholic Church. Sadly this young man would definitely not be admitted into the school."

Clown at Circus Mass Reprimanded for Honking Sanctus Horn at Wrong Part of Consecration

Sources say that just minutes after a Circus Mass at St. Pius X Catholic Church concluded earlier this morning, Pastor and Ring Master Fr. Reggie Smith reprimanded a clown deacon for having honked the horn several seconds after the consecration.

"The GIRM clearly states that 'a little before the Consecration, when appropriate, a server honks a horn as a signal to the audience. According to local custom, the server also honks the horn as the priest and ringmaster shows the host and then the chalice,'" an infuriated Smith told EOTT as he kissed and hung up his ringmaster whip. "And our local custom *is* to honk the horn at this point. After all, what's the point in using the Sanctus Horn if it's not used to alert the faithful of the consecration." Smith added that not even the Pope himself had the right to change the rubrics of the Mass, and that doing so was in complete contradiction to the spirit of obedience.

At press time, Smith said that he will consider administering disciplinary action should this type of negligence happen again in the future.

[News from the Future] Martians Protest during Third Vatican Council

Thousands of New Calcedonian Martians from the northern quadrant of sector 490-3t protested outside New St. Peter's today as bishops began talks on a number of heated issues including inter-species marriage and receiving communion in the pinchers.

"The faithful and bishops alike are hoping to cover all the core issues that the average Catholic Martian on the planet's going through; issues such as understanding 'the fall' in regards to the Martian race, and of course, receiving communion in the pinchers as opposed to one of the three tongues," spokesman for the Church in sectors 490-3t and 490-4t Androm'da Zmit told the press outside New St. Peter's Square. "I have faith that our Holy Father Beeblebrox XV, together with the bishops, will be able to guide the faithful in these decisions...to help them better understand how he, she, or heshe can better telecommunicate the gospel."

One issue receiving lots of attention is that of intergalactic marriage. The question of whether humans could lawfully marry Martians was first thrust into the spotlight when well known intergalactic space hockey player Xed Zardox fell in love with Martian actress Trillion Pan Vogon, causing a storm of controversy. Other issues the bishops are considering are whether it's admissible to form crop circles outside one's own property and whether human probing is to be allowed during Lent.

New California Law Forces Parishes
to Switch to E-Thuribles

A new ban on thurible smoke will take effect in all California churches beginning next year, State officials are now confirming.

The ban, which comes decades after a 1995 ruling that banned all smoking in enclosed workplaces in California, is set to take effect in all Catholic churches across the state. The Governor of California told the press Thursday that he hoped the move would help pastors who consistently used incense during Mass to quit. "But in the end, we know that people have their rights, and some priests will continue to use incense, but this law is to ensure the safety of our children, and those who are adversely affected by the smoke of others."

One proponent of the new law told EOTT this morning that he was happy about the changes coming. "As new parents, my wife, Betty, and I are extremely concerned about second-hand incense," California resident Kevin Hardy told EOTT. "In fact, we've even heard how bad third-hand incense is for children, and we won't even allow our priest friend to hold our child if he's said Mass using incense."

The new e-Thuribles have a small button near the handle, which turns on an atomizer located inside the thurible, and burns what smells like incense, but is in all actuality just vapor. E-Thurible manufacturer *'N Sense* says they are in the process of creating different thurible flavors including Cherry Slurpee, and Bubblegum Mint.

At press time, Bishop Jaime Soto of Sacramento had released a statement in response to the ruling that reads in part, *"What State officials don't understand is that we in California haven't even used a thurible in the past few decades. So who are the suckers now?"*

Man Sits through Entire St. Therese Film; Second John XXIII Miracle Now Confirmed

Murrieta, CA—Just weeks after Pope Francis waived the second miracle requirement for the canonization of Pope John XXIII, the Congregation for the Causes of Saints announced that they have found and approved a miracle attributed to the late pontiff. What the Vatican is calling an "inexplicable surge of supernatural endurance" by a Murrieta man who was able to sit through a viewing of the 2005 film *St. Thérèse* in one sitting has been assessed as a miracle. The unknown Murrieta man prayed to John XXIII halfway through the film and was reportedly given an unexplainable amount of endurance, as well as an unprecedented amount of strength to endure what scientists believe must have been "a couple hours of pure, unadulterated misery." The claim was first taken to scientists and they were not able to explain how someone was able to sit through the film without going absolutely nuts," Bishop Rodrigo Spola of the Congregation for the Causes of Saints told reporters. "We therefore had no other explanation than the miraculous intercession of John XXIII. We've seen some very strange cases in the last few decades, but this one, how you say, takes the cake."

Zombie Apocalypse at Heart of Evangelii Gaudium

In the 224-page Apostolic Exhortation Evangelii Gaudium, Francis has asked those in the Church to become more visionary, more merciful, and to begin packing the necessary items needed to survive the impending zombie apocalypse.

"I dream of a missionary option," Francis writes, "that is capable of transforming everything, so that the Church's customs and ways of doing things can be suitably channeled for the evangelization of today's world. Also, we must think of *tomorrow's* world, and begin preparing for the night of the living dead, when the dead shall rise to feast upon the flesh of the living."

Francis goes on to ask all Catholics to come to a process of conversion, saying that those who are truly disciples will be missionary disciples, characterized by the joy of the faith. "Evangelizers," he says, "must never look like someone who has just come back from a funeral, for indeed, some of those who come back from a funeral in those days may be the very people who were buried."

"But rather," he continues, "we must be those who wish to share the joy of those who have passed, but who have not 'turned,' thanking the Lord for taking them out of such a sad and desolate world and into His merciful arms, who invites others to a delicious banquet [of real food like pizza and donuts], as opposed to human flesh." Francis goes on to describe how the Church must go forth, "building bridges to help men, women, and children escape a horde of walkers," and by supporting others, taking on the smell of the dead so as to hide their scent from the walking dead, and to patiently seek to accompany them on their journey.

"For truly, in those days, we shall all be infected. And when we pass, it will only be a matter of hours before we, too, turn into these animated, yet soulless corpses, prowling about the earth." Francis reminds the faithful that the good news of Christ's resurrection should be the heart of the Gospel: "In the end, we shall all rise in imitation of Christ, who rose and conquered death so that we, too, may rise. But for those whose bodies rise without their souls, we will be called to free them by bullet, sword, hammer, arrow, or bat to the skull. The important thing I'm trying to get through to you, I guess, is that it must be through the brain. You must kill the brain, or else they will just keep coming."

Lapsed Catholic Confirms She Is Still Spiritual

27-year-old Sara Matson confirmed to friends yesterday that she was indeed still very spiritual despite no longer attending Mass.

Matson, a World Religions teacher at St. Francis Xavier Catholic School in Sherman Oaks, California, reported to her friends that she feels her creator's presence everywhere. "Not that there's anything wrong with going to church," Matson later confirmed. "There's also nothing wrong with *not* going to church. And actually, if you really think about it...since our creator, call her what you will, *is in everything*, then really, everywhere is church, if you kinda think about it like that."

At press time, Matson had asked her friends not to judge her, since you don't define another when you judge them, but rather, define yourself.

Family Atheist Disproves Existence of
Grandfather He's Never Seen

As debate continued over whether or not it was appropriate for members of the Hamilton residence to discuss the topic of Grandpa Joe in the home, family atheist Rob Hamilton argued with family members that they had absolutely zero "rock-hard evidence" proving the existence of his so-called "grandpa."

Hamilton told a gathering at the annual Hamilton Family Reunion that he has in fact definitively disproven the existence of his grandfather, and planned to reveal his findings in his new book, *The Grandpa Joe Delusion*. "In my book, I eviscerate the major arguments for the existence of my grandpa and I demonstrate the supreme improbability that we actually have one in the family," Hamilton told family members gathered around a picnic table. "Furthermore, I show how a belief in this supposed grandfather that many of us have never even seen or heard from has fueled turmoil in the family, causing conflicts that would never have arisen if we all accepted that there is no Grandpa Joe. Moreover, I buttress points with proof from Ancestry.com disproving that he is my father's father."

Hamilton went on to ask several members of the family how they could believe in a grandpa who would allow them to suffer while they were having financial troubles in the late 90s. "It is said that he was a wealthy man, a well-renowned watch-maker, and that the watch my father wears was made by him. To this first point I ask, 'Why did he not send us money when we were financially strapped?' To the second, simply because my father's watch is beautiful, there is no reason to believe that just because it is beautiful, that it necessarily had to have been made by him." Hamilton went on to add that all the mentions of Grandpa Joe in the Hamilton Family History book were obviously made up by his own father, who was clearly in a desperate state at the time of the writing of the history. "At the time he wrote the book, our family was immigrating from England, and many did not want to leave. My father needed a way to bring the fear of some wealthy and powerful member of the family demanding that we leave England to actually have them move." Hamilton clinched his argument by asking the irrefutable question, "Who was Grampa Joe's grampa?"

Leaked Documents Reveal NSA Spied on Prayers of Faithful

According to a new report out this week in the Italian magazine *Panorama*, the NSA may have spied on the prayers of millions of faithful during the last Papal Election.

The report states that the agency, which is embroiled in a number of scandals, is believed to have been intercepting prayers within the hearts and minds of millions of Catholics made to God during the conclave that saw Cardinal Jorge Mario Bergoglio elected Pope.

Jesuit Father Frederico Lombardi, Director of the Holy See Press Office, told EOTT today that he was not concerned with the allegations, saying, "We don't know anything about this matter, and seriously doubt that it had any impact on the conclave."

But not all Catholics are taking the news in stride. Just this morning in St. Peter's Square, hundreds of Catholics protested the NSA, calling the NSA's actions "an invasion of privacy."

"They've taken it too far this time!" one protester told reporters. "They spied on our prayers with the idea that if they could understand who Catholics were praying for, that they could get an idea of who was gonna be elected. But I prayed about a lot of personal things during that conclave, and it sickens me to think that people were overhearing those things."

Agency spokesman Vanee Vines told David Gregory on *Greet the Press* this morning that the idea of spying on prayers is "ludicrous." "The National Security Agency did not, and does not target the Vatican. Assertions that the NSA has targeted the Vatican, published in Italy's *Panoramo* magazine, are not true. Case closed. And on a related note; seriously, Kevin Spiegle of Omaha, Nebraska? Burke? You actually thought Burke had a shot? Ha!"

Christendom College Student Won't Shut up with the Latin Already

Friends of Christendom College freshman Ben Tate reported this week that "he hasn't shut up with the whole Latin thing" since returning for spring break.

The 19-year-old undergrad had just recently returned from Front Royal, Virginia for break when friends began to notice there was something different about him. "Well, we knew there was something wrong with him the moment we picked him up from the airport," longtime friend Roger McNerney told EOTT. "When we asked how things were going, he just sat back, took a deep breath and said, 'Deus bonum est, my friends... Deus... bonum...est.'"

McNerney went on to say that he and other friends are suspicious that Tate sometimes just makes up his own Latin, ending English words with -eum and -eus, knowing that no one else knows the language, and therefore cannot call him out on it. "Look...I may not know Latin, but I *do* know BS. I asked him what he thought about the whole North Korea thing and he came back with, 'Well, as Socrates once said, "Situatsionem non est goodum."'"

Man Drops $10 in Donation Basket Like He's Some Kind of Beverly Hills Millionaire

In what many witnesses are calling "a stunning act of generosity," a mysterious parishioner was spotted placing a $10 bill into the donation basket at the St. Mark's Catholic Church 9:00 a.m. Mass as though he were some sort of Beverly Hills millionaire.

"He pulled out a crisp $10 bill from his billfold, snapped it a couple times, folded it in half, and flicked it with his finger as if he hadn't a financial care in the world," witness Randy McGrath told EOTT before going on to say that the mysterious millionaire acted so nonchalant that one could easily have deduced that this was not the first time he had donated such a substantial sum of money.

"I mean, his hands weren't even trembling by the time the basket got to him. He just kinda leaned back in his pew and tossed the bill in the basket from about a half-foot out with the calm and poise of a man who's used to handling large bills. After the basket passed, you could see everyone just kinda looking at the bill and pointing at it. Some people even turned around to see who may've dropped it in."

Observers witnessed the mysterious Beverly Hills Millionaire drive off after Mass in what many described as a lavish 2007 Chevy Malibu.

At press time, the usher in charge of the basket was carefully taking the bill out of the basket and placing it in her bra for safe keeping.

" "He pulled out a crisp $10 bill from his billfold, snapped it a couple times, folded it in half, and flicked it with his finger as if he hadn't a financial care in the world," witness Randy McGrath told EOTT. "

California Lawmakers Pass New Opposite-Sex Marriage Ban

New marriages involving people of the opposite sex will be banned in California under a new bill passed by the State Legislature on Wednesday, and straight couples already married will have to register as "domestic partners."

The measure, which passed the State Assembly 74-1, will now be passed on to the Governor of California for his signature after amendments are approved in the State Senate. This is just one of the bills passed by the senators in the wake of rising tensions between gay marriage advocates and same-sex opponents.

The bill will ban all marriages involving couples with different genital parts, save for those that include a human being and an animal. Those who already are in committed relationships with "non-humans," including animals, plants, and inanimate objects, will still be required to register for marriage licenses.

"We in the LGBT community believe that it was time to take the offensive," said prominent transgender advocate Mr. Giselle Adams. "It's time now to move aggressively toward a world where opposite marriage is a thing of the past. That would certainly help stop the discrimination."

Bills in the package passed by the Senate will introduce other laws, including banning movies and music with love themes involving the opposite sex, unless, in the case of movies and television, those heterosexual love affairs end in tragedy, or where one or the other of the characters realizes he or she is either gay or questioning.

Two other bills remain active from the original package, and are expected to be heard later this week.

One would ban any non-homosexual hugging, and the other would ban people who are not gay, lesbian, bisexual, transgender, or questioning from using public restrooms that are not clearly marked "Bigots."

Archbishop of San Francisco Overjoyed to See City's Devotion to God's Covenant with Noah

The archbishop of San Francisco, Salvatore Cordileone, said Thursday after his installation that he was overjoyed to see that the city had such a devotion to God's covenant with Noah.

"Who knew there could be so many rainbows in one place?" he said, happily, to reporters who had gathered after Mass. The 58-year-old archbishop hopes to work with San Franciscans and all those devoted to the Old Testament pre-deluge patriarch in ceasing California's gay marriage initiative.

The "Brown Note" Proven True Seconds
After "Gather Us In" Begins

The infrasonic sound called the "brown note" that some have said causes people to lose control of their bowels was proven true just seconds after the hymn "Gather Us In" began last Sunday at St. Gerard Parish.

Director of Acoustic Resonance and Church Worship at the Vatican, Michelle Klinsmann, said today that, although the frequency needed to hit the supposed brown note is said to be between 5 and 9 Hz, that the hymn "Gather Us In" "defied science."

"It was fascinating to see that before the church band even began to sing, congregants were already beginning to show signs that the brown note had taken effect," Klinsmann told EOTT. "There wasn't even enough resonance, and yet, some were complaining of nausea while others later reported they had felt their blood pressure rising."

"Once the band began singing, I looked at my husband, and he was becoming pale and clammy," said 29-year-old Martha Bing. "Next thing I know, I was running to the restroom alongside the entire congregation, including our pastor. It was uncontrollable. I just wanted to surrender so that they could just stop."

Reports show that the brown note took hold of every single person in the church except for the band, who had reportedly built an immunity to the hymn.

"It's true," said Music Director Raymond Cleese. "Please excuse my language, but we crapped ourselves for a good month rehearsing this song."

"It's really an interesting phenomena," Klinsmann went on to say. "Every single time the hymn has been sung, people have lost control of their bowels. We just don't hear about it because people are typically so embarrassed that they don't say anything."

Several reports say that the chaos truly began when it was time for Communion. "The church devolved into a scene of absolute madness," one anonymous parishioner recalled. "It was horrible. We didn't know which pews went first or which Eucharistic Minister to go to. Next thing you know the riot police are storming the church to restore order. And on top of all that, no one was there to urge those in a state of mortal sin to go to Communion anyway, so some people clogged up the pews."

Monsignor Alberto Casarella of the Archdiocese's Office of the Liturgy told reporters hours after the Mass that new procedures would be instituted to prevent such mishaps in the future. But no one knows how long lasting the impact of this event may be.

Statue in Cathedral of Our Lady of the Angels Wondering Why Everyone Keeps Laughing at It

The Virgin Mary statue at the entrance of Our Lady of the Angels Cathedral in Los Angeles announced today that it was becoming ever more frustrated, and frankly rather confused, by the amount of mockery it has received since it was first created.

The eight-foot-tall, modern representation of the Virgin Mary told EOTT that ever since it was created in 2002, it has been the butt of jokes, scoffs, and laughs by visitors who pass it, despairingly adding that it has oftentimes wished it could just call in sick.

"I guess I'm just more confused than anything else," the statue said from its station above a pair of bronze doors. "Of course I've never looked at myself, but I'm a statue of the Virgin Mary, you know? How bad can I look? People stare at me as though I look like some kind of veilless Jedi with a boy-cut or something."

Nation's Catholics Demand Better Catechesis to Better Understand What Teachings to Ignore

Thousands of the nation's ill-catechized Catholics protested outside the USCCB headquarters in Washington, D.C. last night, demanding better catechesis so as to better understand what Church teachings they are going to continue to ignore.

24-year-old Tanya Wilkins who spearheaded the protest told reporters that she feels the need for better catechesis because she had for years "unconsciously ignored teachings such as contraception and co-habitation without ever really knowing that the Church was even against such practices."

She went on to tell reporters that ever since she finished reading *The Compendium of the Compendium of the Catechism of the Catholic Church,* she felt she was being called to help enlighten the minds of others who were "unconsciously" denying the teachings of the Church. "Now when I tell people that I only attend Mass on Christmas and Easter, I know it's because I just don't care, and not just out of sheer ignorance of my faith."

Fetus Only a Blob of Tissue,
Says 47-Year-Old Blob of Tissue

While reiterating that a fetus is nothing more than a blob of tissue, a 47-year-old blob of tissue today told a gathering of the Planned Parenthood Clergy Advisory Board that a fetus is only a human being in potential.

"We must remember that until a fetus has a heart and a brain, it is not a human being," said the aged mass of cells, who, despite her age, was lacking a heart and brain herself. The aged mass of cells who was nothing more than a product of conception went on to say that a fetus was nothing more than another part of a pregnant woman's body, "like an appendix."

"When a fetus cannot exist independent of the mother, it cannot be regarded as a separate entity," said the clump of cells, whose very own 53-year-old jobless older brother was currently living at home with his mother. The blob of tissue went on to add that the Church cannot tell a woman what she can and cannot do with her body, and demanded that the Mystical Body of Christ ordain women and permit abortion.

At press time, the heartless, brainless blob of tissue was preparing her speech to federal officials about expanding the critical habitat zone of the California tiger salamander.

Satanic Group to Desecrate Welch's, Wonder Bread, in Mockery of Methodist Church Service

A Harvard University student group plans to host a reenactment of a Satanic Praise and Worship Service on campus Friday night, and a former pastor at a Boston Methodist church says they are tampering with evil.

The plan has drawn criticism from Boston Methodist officials who expressed "deep sadness and strong opposition" to the plan.

The reservation-only event Friday night is scheduled to be held at the Queen's Head Pub at Harvard's Memorial Hall, according to a flyer provided by the student group.

The Harvard Extension Cultural Studies Club said in a statement posted online that it planned to host a historical reenactment of a Black Praise and Worship Service, including the desecration of a 16 oz. bottle of Welch's Grape Juice, as well as a loaf of Wonder Bread.

Pastor of United Methodist Church, Reverend Ron Duncan, said the students would be desecrating the "true symbol of the Lord," and thereby "symbolically condemning their souls."

"The fact is that we believe that Christ is truly present in the Wonder Bread and in the Welch's...and by truly present, I mean, in a truly symbolic way. Does that make sense?" Duncan told EOTT as a tear slid down his cheek, a symbol, as he put it, of his grief.

Leaders of the Harvard Extension Cultural Studies Club re-

sponded today saying that the event Friday is "simply a reenactment, and that some could argue that Praise and Worship is
itself, in some ways, Satanic," because the "monstrosity of the
music is contrary to the concept of God as beauty."

Cardinals Distancing Themselves from Pope Ahead of next Papal Election

Ahead of the next Papal Elections, many cardinals have begun to distance themselves from the Pope, whose approval rating amongst traditional-leaning Catholics is at an all-time low.

As these cardinals are beginning to focus on their possible election to the throne of St. Peter, they are increasingly calculating how close is too close to an unpopular Pope Francis.

The Pope's dismal poll ratings with traditional-minded Catholics could sink many cardinals' hopes for becoming next in line to become Vicar of Christ, especially with battleground bishops and swing cardinals.

"If he is where he is now for the remainder of his papacy, it's not going to work for liberal cardinals who want to impress members of the College of Cardinals on the right," said Cardinal Raymond Burke, who stated earlier this year that he would not seek election during the next conclave. "I think that if the next conclave goes to the right, that it will be more of a referendum on Pope Francis' loose words, than on a conservative agenda."

Some right-leaning cardinals are also keeping their distance from next year's Synod on the Family after recent remarks made by Pope Francis regarding the easing up of the annulment process so that any Catholic wanting an annulment can have one by simply turning to their spouse at any time and saying the words, "thou art banish'd."

Planned Oklahoma City Black Mass Stirring Controversy with Schismatic Satanist Group

The black mass scheduled for September 21 in Oklahoma City is stirring lots of controversy with traditional-minded Satanists, *The Oklahoma City Satanist Weekly* is reporting.

The open invitation "black mass" scheduled to be held at the Civic Center Music Hall is sold-out, but one schismatic Satanic group is calling the upcoming black mass a "sacrilege" against the Prince of Darkness.

Anthony Williams, the leader of the schismatic satanic group *The Society of Beelzebub*, has told EOTT that "the new order of the black mass that will be used on September 21 is illicit."

"These types of all-are-welcome, hippie black masses are not only invalid, but they are a mockery of the true blasphemy of the black mass," Williams said. "The black mass is the most unholy thing on earth and should not be trivialized with some wishy-washy theories about inclusiveness."

When asked why The Society of Beelzebub splintered from the largest Satanist group in the world, Williams said that it all started after the Second Gehenna Council.

"That's where all this satanic modernity stems from. From there we started getting crazy liberal ideas and philosophies like Liberation Demonology that taught that even non-Satanists can enter Hell."

Williams is asking people to boycott the black mass, saying,

"From some fissure, the smoke of God has entered the temple of Satan."

Catholic Democrats Vote in
Referendum to Secede from Catholicism

Catholic Democrats voted to secede from the Catholic Church in a referendum yesterday, with final results showing that 95.5% of ballots were in favor of becoming Pagan.

Leaders from the Pagan Coalition will pass legislation allowing Catholics in the Democratic Party who follow their consciences even when they conflict with moral teachings of the Magisterium, to be known as Pagans. The Vatican has welcomed the results, with the Vatican Press Office today issuing a statement of support and congratulations.

"Results of the referendum in the Democratic Party clearly showed that Catholic Democrats see their future only as part of the Pagan movement," said Vatican Press Secretary Roberto Ansaldi. "We support their decision and hope that their transition will be seamless. 'Transition' isn't the right word there, is it? 'Transition' would imply some sort of change from one position to another."

Parishioner Has Awkward Conversation with Ex-Boyfriend Moments before Receiving Communion from Him

It was reported today that Samantha Ross, ex-girlfriend of local Eucharistic Minister Donny King, accidentally ran into her one-time fiancé as she received communion from his hands during Mass early this morning.

"That was real awkward," said longtime friend of Ross, Kelly Lions, who was standing behind her in the communion line. "She was there talking to him for like five minutes. Before he recognized her, he said, 'The Body of...' then realized it was Samantha. That's when it got awkward. He asked how she'd been doing and she asked him the same. They were very polite, very cordial, and both asked whether the other was seeing anyone and how their parents were. Honestly, though, most awkward time I've ever experienced waiting in line for communion."

Lions also reported that the conversation lasted for some five minutes as everyone in line cringed at the awkwardness of the two bumping into one another.

Ross later reported to EOTT that the incident would've been "just fine" had King not brought up the issue that the two had constantly fought about before their breakup.

"Typical Donny," Ross said. "I told him I wasn't seeing anyone and he just smiled in that obnoxious passive-aggressive way that he does when he doesn't believe you. That's when I screamed at him and the next thing you know, there we are

yelling back and forth at each other in the middle of communion, but no one was looking, of course, cause they've dealt
with these screaming matches in the middle of Mass before. I
even saw Fr. Brian tip-toeing around the altar and whispering
the final blessing so that everyone could get the heck out before
it really got bad. Whatever. I'll receive communion next week."

Rare Species of Bird Found Nesting
in Mark Shea's Beard

A team of scientists studying in the remote backwoods of Mark Shea's beard announced the discovery of a rare species of bird found nesting behind little rocks and foliage found in the red bush of the 57-year-old Catholic apologist.

According to biologists, the sixth–month expedition into the dangerous wastelands of Shea's beard, in which two scientists have already died, has produced various exciting discoveries.

"We're all so excited with what we've been able to find in this treacherous and uncharted territory of Mark Shea's face," lead biologist Ben Ringle told EOTT. "Along with this rare species of bird, we've located other types of hair unusual in these parts. We've found other red hair that we believe can be traced all the way back to Jimmy Akin's face, as well as hints of lush brown, not uncommon in the regions of Patrick Madrid's upper lip. How this has happened, we're not sure. It's like a modern day Stonehenge."

We've found other red hair that we believe can be traced all the way back to Jimmy Akin's face, as well as hints of lush brown, not uncommon in the regions of Patrick Madrid's upper lip.

Iraqi Christian Who Risks Life to Attend Mass Not Super Concerned about Bad Church Music Right Now

Iraqi Christian Raghda Ablahad and three other family members risked their lives to attend Sunday Mass in Tel Keppe, Iraq this week. Ablahad reported to family members that Catholics around the world were, at that very moment, "no joke," complaining about female altar servers, as well as the music at Mass.

Ablahad told family members that, though she herself was not a big fan of the music played at her church, she had decided to spend her free time on the "little things," like finding a less-conspicuous route to church, and watching her back for radical Muslims looking to slay an infidel for Allah.

When asked *when* she had decided to stop focusing on the bad church music and the fact that her church had female altar servers, Ablahad told EOTT: "If I had to take a guess, that would probably be the moment I saw Muslim militants pointing guns at my child's head...yes...I think that was the moment."

Q&A With the Man Behind Eye of the Tiber, S.C. Naoum

Tell us how it all started?

The site was created as a way for me to vent and to hopefully evangelize. I don't know what, if any, success I've achieved with the latter, but I think I've done one heck of a job with the former. I have to admit that when I say I wanted to use this site partly as a vehicle to evangelize, I didn't actually expect more than family and perhaps some friends to visit the site. So I was pleasantly surprised and a bit caught off-guard when Catholic bloggers began following the site and reposting articles. Then some bloggers began writing about EOTT and I was being asked to do interviews. That's when I knew I really had to start watching what I said, because people I didn't know were actually reading this crap. And with that there came an interesting evolution in the composition of the articles. When I had just begun writing, I was very bold and not so subtle. After all, it was just family and some friends visiting the site. Once I realized that the public was actually visiting the site, I toned down my style so as not to offend. I wasn't simply out to offend for the sake of offending and getting a reaction, but to simply be honest in the message I was trying to deliver. I knew by then that I couldn't please everyone. There would always be that guy who thought I'd gone too far. Almost every single article written has been followed by a comment or email by "that guy." But for every "that guy," there are many more readers who wish I would've gone harder. I'm confident now more than ever in my approach to writing articles. I write what comes, when it comes, however it comes. It's certainly different than when I began writing. And I think readers appreciate the spontaneity and the sometimes bold approach I have to take if an article's gonna work. Those are the thick-skinned Catholics that I target; the ones I know are gonna stick with the site because they understand and appreciate that the nature of satire sometimes means you can't hold back.

Why satire?

There's no other form so conducive to exposing absurdity than satire. With satire, you're given the freedom to exaggerate truths, make up quotes, characters, and alternate storylines to amplify the absurdity of what you're reporting. In fact, you're not so much given the freedom to do so as you are forced to. Satire cannot be dry as you see in a typical newspaper, unless it's a calculated move. You must take the form of the typical newspaper article, which is painstakingly humdrum to read, but then you get to spice it up with a splash of bedlam. That's what I love about satire; the havoc and mania hidden beneath the guise of "proper" reporting. When you write a proper article about the pope saying this or the Vatican doing that, you do so by delivering the facts and nothing but the facts. With an opinion piece you're given the freedom to give your opinion on the matter at hand. Satire sits somewhere in the middle. You deliver the same information as provided in a news report or opinion piece, but you're also given the opportunity to be a little more creative. You're given the opportunity to make your readers laugh, even if the subject being satirized is a frustrating one. More important than anything, though, is the fact that I take great pride in newer readers not understanding that an article is a joke.

What was the initial reception like, and when did things start to pick up?

I remember that some months after beginning the site, several prominent Catholic writers started linking to my page. The reception was great. Well, maybe it was just good, but in my head it was great. So let's go with great, yeah? Some of my fondest memories of those early days were the fears I had of being reprimanded by some angry priest or bishop. But then I started hearing from many priests and even a large number of bishops telling me that they really enjoyed my work and encouraged me to keep it up. Perhaps it wasn't a large number of bishops, but again, let's just go with what's in my head. Anyhow, I once tried to think about which article it was that really launched EOTT, but nothing particularly stood out as the definitive article. It was, and continues to be, more of an organic growth. Years after beginning the site, I still consider it in a constant state of "picking up." I believe that the site is still launching, and I think that's the best way to go about growing EOTT. It's not like a novel, which, once published, is complete whether the author likes it or not. A site can continue to mature. And that's why I never plan on doing something stupid like publishing an Eye of the Tiber book.

What is your main goal with EOTT?

I'd like to continue to make Catholics laugh. Or for those Catholics (friends and family included) who do not laugh at my articles, I'd like to start making them do so. But the goal is not simply laughter, but proclaiming the Good News. I've always considered EOTT an apostolate wearing a clown nose. There're far too many days where I wake up and find out this or that absurd thing is happening in the Church and can't help but to laugh. If I didn't laugh, I'd probably spend most of my time in the corner of the bathroom crying. But since my wife hates when I do that, and would rather see me off to work, I laugh. This is great insight into who I am, by the way. If you ever run across me laughing, know that inside, there's a very good chance I'm crying. But I digress. I think a lot of people in the Church feel the way I do. I think that priests and laity alike expect so much from those who "run" the Church that we sometimes overreact to things. Sometimes, we don't overreact at all, but whether frustration is warranted or not, my goal is to continue giving Catholics a voice and an outlet. A place where they can go to vent and laugh at the same time.

What helps you decide what to write about?

I've said this so much that I think it's become cliche, but my answer is whiskey. I think it was Hemingway who said, "write drunk, edit sober." Now, I don't get drunk because I find it difficult to write while everything is spinning, but I don't mind thinking up ideas while drinking. But those are sometimes the dangerous articles. Sometimes I think up a headline at night that I'm pleased with and go to bed excited to know what I'm gonna write about the next day. Then I wake up and realize that the whiskey I drank the previous night must've been 90 proof, because my headline idea is out of control or altogether unintelligible. Whiskey aside, the majority of my ideas come while I'm at Mass. I don't consciously try to think up ideas there, but they come. There I am praying and next thing you know I'm wondering whether a clown at a Circus Mass would be reprimanded if he were to honk the Sanctus Horn at the wrong part of the consecration. I probably come up with five ideas every Mass. Most of them end up being stupid, which makes me really frustrated because I spent so much time focusing on trying to get the idea out of my head so I can pray, just to not use the idea in the end. EOTT is having a negative impact on my prayer life during Mass. I think I'm just gonna shut the site down.

One Catholic voice you could meet, who would it be and why?

Are we talking dead or alive? If it's either, I go Chesterton. If you have to ask why, then you clearly haven't read *Orthodoxy* or *The Everlasting Man* or literally anything else he ever wrote. If I was to choose someone living, it's would hands down have to be Pope Benedict. Mainly because I'd like to know that I got to meet a living saint and Doctor of the Church. And I won't even say that I'd pick his brain about the Church or prayer. I'd simply sit there and listen. And if he wasn't talking, I'd simply stare at him until he turned to look at me, at which time I'd hastily look down to my lap. In the meantime, I'd be trying to figure out a way to cut off a small piece of his hair. And I would take the hair and place it in a little reliquary, so that I could one day venerate it.

What's the future hold for EOTT?

That's a tough question. I'd be blessed to just see it continue to grow. I don't really care much for growing it into something as big as The Onion. If I get close to that that's fine, but to do that, I'm afraid I'd have to target the masses, which I fear would take away from the familiar, family-like (sometimes) atmosphere the site has now. What it will develop into in ten or twenty years, I have no idea. All I know is that as long as I am able to continue this silly little apostolate, and make a few people laugh along the way, I'll consider EOTT a success.

ABOUT THE AUTHOR

S.C. NAOUM is the founder and Chief Executive Oligarch of Eye of the Tiber. He invented satire at the age of five while solving a Rubik's Cube blindfolded, and is the first Catholic in history to be canonized and made Doctor of the Church while still alive. He is a legendary Thomist who is able to out-Thomas Thomas himself. He has been known to out-meditate a Trappist, out-teach a Dominican, out-Catholic the Pope, out-pious Piuses one through twelve put together with his hands tied behind his back. He is currently drinking whiskey.